A Horse by Any Other Name

He turned away, as if he couldn't stand the very sight of me. I tried to hurry on, but Charlie was tiring and I heard Mum calling out anxiously, 'Fran, is everything all right? D'you think you can make it?'

To save the poor neglected chestnut, Charlie, that was the thing. But Fran was worrying about the handsome stranger who had helped her yet followed her with contempt in his eyes.

Fran had to concentrate on the horse – he needed her love. But the stranger...what did *he* need?

JENNY HUGHES is an established short-story writer whose work has appeared in numerous magazines. Here she has combined her knowledge of horses with her considerable talent for romantic teenage fiction.

Also in this series: The Dark Horse

A
HORSE BY ANY
OTHER NAME
Jenny Hughes

KENILWORTH PRESS

For Donna and Rachael Bradbury
With my love

First published in Great Britain 1994
The Kenilworth Press Limited
Addington, Buckingham, MK18 2JR

© Jenny Hughes 1994

British Library Cataloguing in Publication Data
A catalogue record for this book is available from the British Library.

ISBN 1-872082-55-6

Typeset in ITC Bookman 9/12 by
The Kenilworth Press Limited
Printed by Hollen Street Press, Berwick upon Tweed

ONE

Looking back it gives me a strange feeling to realise that I saw both Charlie and Kez for the first time on the very same day. Then, of course, I had no way of knowing how important they would both become or how intertwined our lives would be – though there wasn't much intertwining that first day. But, I'd better start at the beginning instead of the middle and tell you how Charlie came about.

I live with my mum, who's a fairly successful writer. She writes what I think are pretty obscure novels, and she's very scatty and disorganised and impulsive but a really brilliant person. She and my dad are divorced because they both say she's impossible to live with. I get on OK with Dad and visit him regularly, and just occasionally I agree with the verdict on living with Mum. The day I'm on about was one of those times.

We live in an ordinary house, but it's got its own land and we're lucky enough to have a couple of paddocks and a small stable block.

Two years ago, when the Charlie and Kez day happened, we were pottering along in our slightly offbeat but perfectly happy way with my pony mare, Brontë, and Mum's loopy Anglo-Arab, Woolf, and the dogs, cats, chickens and pig who make up the rest of our family. (I'll tell you about the pig later.)

Anyway, there was I, singing along to the radio in the kitchen, cooking the hens' mash and trying to stop Shelley, our brainless terrier, from coming in through the cat-flap, when in flew Mum, all wild hair and flashing eyes.

'Come on, Fran, help me hitch up the trailer. I've never been so angry in my life!'

I turned out the gas under the hens' saucepan and

firmly removed Shelley from the cats' dinner. 'Where are we going?' I was already pulling on my boots. I'm used to sudden crises.

'The other side of the village. I was coming back from town on the lower road and there was a horse tethered on some grass verge past the housing estate. He looked...he looked *awful*, Fran. I just wept when I saw him.'

'Hang on,' I said, alarmed. 'What are you planning to do, kidnap it? Even if it is in a bad way you can't do that.'

She looked round wildly. 'We'll need a decent head-collar and lead rope and a feed bucket and...'

'Already in the trailer.' I keep everything like that together. 'But Mum, I told you, we can't just go and steal the horse...'

'Steal?' She kicked off her going-to-town shoes and started hunting around. 'Don't be silly.'

'Your wellies are in the porch,' I said, with as much patience as I could manage. 'But, Mum...'

'I've bought him.' She wouldn't meet my eye, which is always a sign she knows she's been rash.

'Oh, *MOTHER*,' I began.

'Fran, when you see him you'll understand. The brute who owns him...I threatened him with the police, RSPCA, everybody. He just sneered and said he'd move his cara-van and the horse so they wouldn't find him, and he *would*. The poor, poor animal. He's in such distress I had to do *something*.'

'So you bought him.' I threw my hands up in despair. 'You handed over our month's housekeeping, did you? If the man's that sort of rogue do you really think the horse will still be there when you get back? He'll take the money and the horse *and* push off like he said.'

'Give me some credit.' She gave me a reproachful look. 'I gave him the cash and took the horse up the road to Dr Jefferies. He's got that old empty stable in the back. He

6

let me put the chestnut in there and said he'd keep an eye on him till we brought the trailer.'

I was torn between total annoyance and a grudging admiration for the way she gets things done. Dr Jefferies is a real old misery, but she'd got even him joining in.

'OK.' I shrugged and headed for the car. 'But what are we going to do with a broken-down old horse when we do get him home? You said we couldn't afford another horse anyway.'

'Fran, for a fourteen-year-old you're sadly cynical.' She'd put on her wellies without changing out of her tailored suit and looked more eccentric than ever. 'I don't think the chestnut is old, just badly treated and under-fed. And I can't afford him but I certainly can't leave him there. I thought we could take care of him, get him well and fit, then sell him to a good home. That's if you don't want him, of course.' She gave me a hopeful look but I was still totally disapproving and wouldn't smile back.

'Mmm, he sounds just what I want. And I'm nearly fifteen by the way. A run-down horse rescued from a gypsy. If he's broken at all he's probably ruined, unrideable and unmanageable. Absolutely ideal.'

'I sometimes think you've got no heart, no feelings at all.' She ran a hand through her great mop. 'Blast this hair. I was so upset when I saw what a state the horse was in I ran across the field to the man's caravan and pulled out all the pins going through the hedge.'

'And you ruined your best shoes.' I was being horrible but she really was a bit much. *She* was supposed to be bringing *me* up, so how come I was the one behaving like a grown-up? 'Come on then, before old Jefferies starts charging us rent on that loosebox of his.'

Shelley leapt into the car, followed by Sam, our labrador, and Mum backed it up so we could hitch the trailer on. She thundered out of the yard and I had to remind her to take it steady – at that speed we were swaying dizzily. It took only a few minutes to get to the doctor's house and he was in his garden, waiting to help Mum manoeuvre into his drive.

I left them to it and walked round to the old stable at the back of the house. I was steeling myself to be hard about this rescued, but to me unwanted, horse but I wasn't prepared for the look of blank despair in the dark eyes of the rough chestnut head looking out at me.

He'd been tethered in a halter so tight it had rubbed off all the hair underneath it and there were sores, some old, some fresh and bleeding, where it had cut into his skin. The hair that was left was dull and staring and his mane was filthy and matted. I'd stuffed my pockets full of pony nuts and I held some on the flat of my palm as I approached him quietly. He dropped his nose and scooped them eagerly into his mouth.

I kept talking softly and went into the stable to look him over. It was dark in there but even in that dim light I could see the outline of his ribs against the rough coat, his tucked-up and miserable appearance, untended sores and cuts, and the deep poverty lines that showed on his quarters.

'You poor, poor baby.' I was fighting back tears. I try to be tough in front of Mum; she's so passionate I have to play everything down to get some balance into our lives, but I really can't bear to see animals suffering, and undoubtedly this chestnut horse had been doing just that. 'How long has that swine been keeping you tied up on a bit of rope?'

I fed him some more pony nuts and stroked him gently. His eyes already looked less blank and he actually leant against me, as if grateful for some kindly company.

The car and trailer were outside now and Mum brought one of Woolf's headcollars over to us. 'You see? I had to buy him, didn't I?' she said pleadingly, and I nodded, the tears too close to risk speaking. 'I had to cut the halter off him.' Her hands were trembling I noticed. 'D'you think he can bear to have this headcollar on?'

I took a deep breath and hoped my voice would be cool and normal. 'I'll pad it up with a bandage.'

I wrapped the webbing in the soft fabric and gently slid the headcollar on, talking softly all the time and rewarding the horse with more food. He let me lead him out docilely enough, but when I tried taking him up the ramp he broke into an immediate sweat, rolled his eyes and clamped his back feet rigidly, totally panic-stricken. Mum tried coaxing him with a tempting feed bucket but the horse was too terrified even for that. Old Dr Jefferies suggested giving him a good switch across the backside but we didn't even bother putting him right.

'He's been through the mill in more ways than one,' Mum said and looked ruefully at the trailer. 'There's no way we're going to get him in there, he's been frightened to death at some time.'

'I still say give him a whack,' Dr Jefferies, grumpy old devil, said. 'You'll have to shift him soon whichever way you do it. I don't want him here.'

I looked round at Mum and she shrugged her shoulders apologetically. 'I'll lead him,' I said. 'It's not far and he'll be OK if I take it steady.'

'I'll follow you.' She gave me a grateful smile. 'In case you have any problems.'

The chestnut horse walked out willingly enough, glad, no doubt, to be away from the frightening trailer and the gloomy old stable. It also helped that I was still bribing him with pony nuts. I led him along the lane and I remember hoping, somewhat snobbily, that none of the girls from school would pass. We looked such a sight. The horse was a decent size, 15.2 or 15.3, but just skin and bone with cracked feet and sparse coat, the long mane and tail clogged and filthy. The bandage-wrapped head-collar made him look like a war casualty, which didn't help.

He walked out beautifully, though, poor battered head in line with my shoulder, not pulling forward or hanging back. I walked on the road and kept him on the grass verge to try and avoid making his feet sore.

I could hear our car purring away behind us and the occasional rattle as the empty trailer hit a bump. The chestnut horse flicked his ears at the sound but he didn't shy or spook and, most surprisingly, he didn't yank at the rope to try and get at the grass or the hedgerows for food.

'You are very well mannered for such a refugee,' I told him admiringly. He didn't answer (of course) but he seemed to like the sound of my voice and the beautiful, though dirt-encrusted eyes were definitely more hopeful.

I kept on chatting as we walked, telling him about our house with its barn and stables, its hen coop and pigsty.

'One thing you'll find odd.' We were approaching a minor crossroads and I was pleased to note the calm way he regarded the traffic we had to cross. 'Well, more than one thing, I dare say, but you will notice something a little strange when we introduce you to all the other animals.' We crossed the road easily and were now in the lane leading to the housing estate and on to our house. 'About half our family have nice, normal names. You've met Sam – I called him that – he's our labrador and he's in the car with Mum and Shelley. Now Shelley seems a pretty average name for a terrier till you realise Mum called him that after the poet.'

I paused and looked at him thoughtfully. 'In fact, if you're going to be staying a while, I'd better do something about a name for you now. Mum got at the other horses before I could have my say, and we ended up with Brontë and Woolf. I don't mind Brontë so much, it quite suits

10

her, but Woolf – I ask you! He's a very good-looking, quite beefy bay and people are always asking why we call him after the stringy grey animal, whereas in fact Mum called him that after Virginia – Virginia Woolf, obviously, one of her favourite writers. When I tell you we've got a bantam cock called Byron and two cats called Pinter and Ayckbourn after the playwrights you see the depth of the problem.' I sighed deeply, and the chestnut flicked an ear towards me. 'I do my best. Most of the hens have normal, non-literary names and I called our other cat, he's the rescue one – he'll only live out of doors – Willow, as in pussy willow, get it?' The horse didn't register anything that time and I went on, 'Mmm, Mum didn't think it was that great either, but I like it. So what can I say is *your* name? You know she's probably dreaming up something for you as we speak. Driving behind us and watching your poor skinny little rump and wondering whether you'd be better as Shakespeare or Ibsen, or even Chekhov.'

He stumbled slightly and I stopped and ran my hand down his leg. 'Poor boy. Not far now. We're nearly at the housing estate and we're only five minutes or so past there. Are your feet hurting, or was it the thought of being called Shakespeare that made you slip?'

He took some more pony nuts, nibbling my palm gently, and I crooned and stroked him to encourage him onward. I was trying to think of the names of chestnut horses I'd known: Firecrest and Rufus, Autumn Gold, Flame and Ruby Star.

'You certainly don't look like any of those.' We continued walking and I looked at him again. He really was a sight. 'You're more of a Battered Beanpole than a Ruby Star.'

He plodded on, not caring. We were approaching the houses now, and to my dread I saw there was a group of youths gathered by one of the garden walls. I gripped the lead rope more tightly, hoping whoever they were, they wouldn't yell or laugh when they saw us and frighten the horse again. I kept on talking, as much to calm my nerves as his. I don't know any of the kids in our village; I go to a girls-only school a few miles away, and most from the village estate go to a big comprehensive nearby. I used to get all hot and nervous when I came upon a gang of them like this. They think I'm stuck up and snobby because I go to a different school and don't live on the estate. And because we've got horses, I suppose. I tried to keep my voice steady as we got nearer and nearer the gathering.

'So what's it to be, then?' I couldn't think of anything else to talk about and the chestnut horse appeared not to mind the old name game. 'Not Beanpole Bert. Skinny Simon? Pathetic Peter? Bit cruel those. How about nice, plain old Charlie? If you smarten up really well we could always refer to you as Charles, couldn't we?'

There were five boys slouching around on the wall, all about my age. Four I knew by sight, rough individuals who loved to cat-call and take the mickey whenever they saw me. The other one was new to me, new to the village I thought, and for a brief moment I looked into brilliant blue eyes set in a dark, good-looking face. My heart was thumping loudly, with fear at the thought of the teasing I was going to get, but in that instance it did an extraordinary lurch of something that wasn't fright.

'Yah! What do we have here?' The biggest of the five, Jake somebody, was mincing around, holding his nose and pretending to be me. 'Little Miss Snot and her gee-gee. Been to the gymkhana, sweetie?'

Not someone who knows that much about horses, as you can tell. The others joined in, blocking our path and making stupid comments in high, affected accents, presumably mimicking mine. I heard Mum wind the window down and shut my eyes, praying she wouldn't say

12

anything embarrassing.

The new one, the one I'd heard them call Kez, didn't join in the tormenting. He just said, in a surprisingly deep voice, 'Let her through. The horse will probably fall down if you don't.'

The gang parted immediately and I looked at Kez gratefully. To my horror the blue eyes were steely cold, the expression on his handsome face one of total, unmistakable scorn.

'Thank you,' I stammered, and he curled his lip and turned away as if he couldn't stand the very sight of me. I tried to hurry on but Charlie was tiring and I heard Mum calling out anxiously 'Fran, is everything all right? D'you think you can make it?'

I nodded, too upset by the encounter with Kez to reply. We plodded slowly on, me and the thin, neglected horse in his bandaged headcollar, until we turned, thankfully and gratefully, into our drive, and were home.

TWO

THERE ARE FOUR looseboxes in our little yard: one for Woolf, one for Brontë, one we use as a tack-room, and a spare. The spare's been useful for visitors or as a sickbay for injured or sick animals and I always make sure it's kept clean with new straw airing and a clean bucket ready for water, and so on. I led Charlie straight to it, and Mum rushed over, still wild-haired and towny-dressed, to shake up a lovely deep bed and put in a big fat haynet. I gently removed the headcollar, showed Charlie where everything was and left him to rest. The yard looks out across to the winter paddock and I thought he'd be comforted to see our two horses, wearing warm New Zealand rugs, happily grazing away.

Mum was on the phone in the kitchen. She'd pinned up some of her hair and kicked off one wellie but she still looked odd. She plonked the receiver back and gave me a relieved grin and a big, big hug.

'You were fabulous! What would I do without you? Did those boys give you trouble? I was just getting out of the car to sort them...'

'No, no trouble.' I pushed away the look of sheer hatred and contempt that Kez had levelled at me. 'That lot always take the mick.'

'Put it down to ignorance.' She hugged me again. 'Horses are something they don't understand, that's all. I've called the vet. He was just on his way out so he'll include us in his visits. I've asked him to take a thorough look at the chestnut. I just hope the poor little beast isn't too far gone to be helped.'

I was so shocked I managed to forget Kez's face for a minute. 'Too far gone? Charlie?'

'You can't call him *Charlie* for goodness sake, Fran.'

She was getting changed into her usual gear of old jods and sweater.

'It's his name,' I said quickly. 'He likes it. But surely he just needs some good grub and his feet and coat seeing to?'

'I certainly hope so. But if worm infestation has taken its toll or there's been bone damage to his legs...'

Considering I'd been so against her buying Charlie and so embarrassed at being seen with him, I felt strangely protective towards the scraggy gelding.

'I'm sure he'll be OK,' I said. 'He's got a lovely nature. Still very sweet considering what he must have been through.'

She gave me an amused glance. 'Hmm. Whatever happened to tough little 'we-don't-want-the-old-nag' Fran? You two certainly seem to have clicked on your walk home.'

'I only said he has a nice disposition.' Immediately, I was defensive. 'That doesn't mean I want to keep him.'

'Oh,' her face fell. 'We'll have to see what the vet says, I suppose. Maybe he'll know someone who'll take the horse.'

'Oh no, I'd like to get him back to rights first.' The thought of the despair in Charlie's kind brown eyes as he was handed over yet again made me feel quite shaky.

Mum patted my back fondly. 'You are odd. I think you enjoy the looking after and handling of horses more than you do the riding part.'

'As much as, anyway,' I agreed. 'I'm not like you, wanting to do cross-countries and hunter trials and thoroughly enjoying loony old Woolf being loony. Brontë's well schooled and well behaved and I know where I am with her.'

'So you'll nurse...um...Charlie back to health and when he's fighting fit and raring to go you'll let someone else have the fun of riding him?' She ran her fingers through her recently tamed hair, making it stand out like a mop again.

I handed her a hair-band. 'Tie it back. I'm going to

keep Charlie company until the vet gets here.'

'OK.' She was being unusually meek, still feeling guilty about parting with the housekeeping, I think.

I went back to the stable and stood close to Charlie as he pulled eagerly at the sweet-smelling meadow hay. He was already warmer to the touch and I longed to get cracking on bathing his sores and cuts and sorting out the tangles in his mane and tail. But Mum wanted the vet to see him as he was and get advice on what to do next, so I carried on petting and talking, and Charlie carried on munching and listening and we both enjoyed it. There was a cloud of worry hovering over me in case the horse was pronounced unsaveable, but when the vet arrived to give him the once-over that was dispelled. The other cloud spoiling my day was the look of scorn on Kez's face, but that one wouldn't go away.

Still, the main fret, Charlie's health, was something I could sort out – that was the good news. We had lotions and creams for the cuts, a diet sheet that would bring joy to any horse's face if he could read, and Charlie received, quite stoically, an antibiotic injection to help fight infection.

'He's basically OK. Keep him on box rest in the warm till the wormers have worked – a week at least – then he can go out for an hour or two when there's some sun to warm his back.' Mr Farrell, our super smashing vet, patted Charlie's rump kindly. 'He's young, only six, and that helps. I'd say before the start of this winter he'd been properly cared for. He's well made too, so once the spring grass comes through and you've got your farrier to sort these feet out, I think you'll be surprised. He seems a nice chap, too.'

I put my arm round Charlie's skinny neck and hugged him gently. 'He is. I can't believe how good-natured he still is. He deserves to feel strong and well again.'

'And you can do it, Fran.' Mr Farrell grinned at me and

16

pulled my short hair teasingly. 'A real natural, that's you. I've seen you bring some pretty hopeless cases back to life so I'm confident about this young man. Anyone else and I'd be worried, but you...'

I felt myself go all pink and silly. Mr Farrell had always encouraged me when I'd cared for Willow, badly injured when thrown out of a passing car, Shelley, savagely bitten by other dogs in his former owner's pack, and an assortment of injured wildlife; but to say I was good enough to save a *horse*, that was really something.

Mum grinned wickedly at the vet. 'Letting Fran know *that* is the equivalent of telling any other female she's beautiful.'

I told you she says embarrassing things sometimes.

Mr Farrell's used to her and just ruffled my hair again and said, 'Oh, she's that too. Goes without saying. Now, do you want me to write all my instructions down, Nurse, or will you remember them all?'

'I'll remember.' I waved the bit of paper with the feeds he'd recommended for Charlie. 'I'll need some dosh for this lot though, Mum.'

'No problem,' she said airily.

'Oh yeah?' I muttered so the departing vet couldn't hear. 'Gonna use the housekeeping, are you?'

I laughed my head off at her outraged face and once she realised I was getting my own back she chased me across the yard with a broom.

We fell through the kitchen door in a giggling heap, just remembering to wave goodbye to Mr Farrell. I could see that he was shaking his head, as if in disbelief, as he drove away. At nearly fifteen you're allowed to clown about but Mum's that bit older, so it takes people by surprise. I was amazingly happy; the irritation when Mum had come rushing into the house earlier had gone and I was glad I'd got such a kind, if slightly batty, mother.

Now I knew we could get Charlie right I couldn't wait to

17

start the treatment – mainly good grub, loads of vitamins, a proper clean-up – and of course lots of that magic ingredient TLC (Tender Loving Care, for those who haven't tried it). The only gloom was the memory of that filthy look from Kez – but there again, I told myself, I'd probably never see him again, so why bother about it?

It was getting near tea-time, both for us and our animal family – quite a performance, as you can imagine. Mum mixed all the feeds while I brought Woolf and Brontë in. They stay out all the time in the summer, but at this time of year they look forward to their nice warm stable and are always waiting by the gate. I took them over to the yard and put them in their boxes. Woolf immediately stuck his nose over the door to have a good look at his new neighbour.

Charlie's scruffy head with its bald patches and sores looked even worse next to Woolf's handsome bay face, but he whickered in a pleased and friendly way, and Woolf didn't seem to mind having this beat-up tramp of a horse next door. Brontë, as usual, merely wanted her rugs changed, her evening wash and brush-up and her lovely bucket of feed, so she gave Charlie one glance and obviously dismissed him from her thoughts.

I must admit I whizzed through the routine quickly so I could spend a little extra time with my new patient. Charlie really was a sweetie, very gentle and easy to handle. He let me pick out his feet, holding up each cracked and chipped hoof patiently. I washed his face with a new soft sponge, and cleaned all the cuts, scratches and weals I could find. He flinched a few times, but let me apply all the soothing ointments Mr Farrell had left, and even nuzzled my hair gently as I bathed his knees. I thought one of Woolf's stable rugs would fit him, but was worried it would rub and chafe the sore skin even further.

'I think he'll be all right without that.' Mum watched

me hover indecisively with the rug. 'He's probably spent all winter out in the cold on that length of rope so it'll be sheer heaven in here for him. The bedding will keep him warm and he'll have decent food inside him for once.'

'I think you're right.' I refolded the rug and scratched him behind the ears. 'I'm dying to have a go at this terrible mane and tail, Charlie boy, but I think you can do without too much pulling about on your first night. Shall I give him his feed and leave him now, Mum?'

'You're the expert.' She crossed her eyes at me in a particularly unlovely way. 'But, yes, I think that's the thing to do. I'm sure he looks better already, Fran.'

'He looks happier,' I amended cautiously. 'It'll take a few weeks before he actually looks *better.*'

Charlie's ears pricked up in amazement as I carried the feed bucket in, and when I tipped it into the scrubbed-out manger he practically nosedived after it. We left him joyfully munching, said goodnight to the other horses, and to Logic, the pig (I *will* tell you about him later, honest), and went indoors to do the dogs' and cats' suppers. Oh, and ours.

We spent the rest of the evening working out a programme to include nursing Charlie. Mum tries to spend as much of the day as possible writing, and of course I've got school, so fitting in all the chores plus exercising Brontë and Woolf, took quite a bit of juggling. Sam and Shelley always come with us when we ride, so they get their walk, or mostly run, at the same time.

'Thank goodness the lighter evenings are on the way,' I said with feeling. 'We were pushed to get everything done before dark even a month ago but Charlie's arrived in time to get the spring grass and more time from us.'

'He'll have to be mostly your baby,' Mum said and ran her hand worriedly through her tied-back hair.

'You look like an explosion in a pillow factory now,' I

19

said and handed her a brush. 'That's fine. I like looking after sick animals – you know I do – so stop fretting. You did the right thing in rescuing him and I'm sorry I was so beastly about it.'

She hugged me. She does that a lot.

'Thanks, Fran. I know I'm a pain but we really had to help him, didn't we?'

''Course we did.' I said. 'And Charlie's already grateful, I can tell.'

'Charlie!' She threw up her hands. 'I know you don't appreciate my literary names, but fancy calling him that. You've got no imagination, none at all.'

'And *you've* got far too much.' I grabbed the brush she was waving around and attacked her hair. 'I'll take the clippers to this lot if you don't keep it under control.'

She submitted to my brushing and scratched the blissfully sleeping Sam with her toe. 'I wonder what...Charlie...will be like to ride? I'm getting Ben to do his feet before we let him into the field next week. Mr Farrell says his legs are sound; it's just sore heels and generally neglected hooves that made him stumble.'

Ben Sandford is our farrier, another terrific person. I must admit really nice people always like my mum, which is heartening. Now I was over my sulk at her impetuousness I liked her a lot myself. In fact I went to bed that night with a lovely, glowing feeling, loving my life and my family, and thinking how contented our new member Charlie had looked when we checked him last thing. He'd whickered a soft greeting and touched my face briefly with his nose, like they do when they recognise a friend.

The only image that spoilt my dreams as I drifted into sleep was the dark, glowering stare from the best-looking face I'd ever seen.

'Forget him,' I told myself hazily. 'You'll probably never see that Kez again.'

THREE

BUT I COULDN'T have been more wrong. I saw him the very next day in fact, though only briefly and at a distance, it's true. Mum spotted him first. We'd been riding in the morning, it being Saturday, and were turning Brontë and Woolf back out into the winter paddock.

'Isn't that one of the boys who got in your way yesterday?' Mum said, pointing to where a lean figure was standing by the fence in the far corner.

I screwed up my eyes (she's got better long sight than me) and peered. 'It's Kez.' I did a cross between a yelp and a gulp.

She looked at me. 'I've never heard you mention him before. Who is he?'

'I don't know.' I pretended to fiddle around with Brontë's New Zealand. 'I saw him for the first time yesterday when you did.'

'I hope he's not going to cause any bother.' She looked anxiously at the fence. 'We're all post-and-rail so he can't let the horses out or anything. I wonder, should I chase him off?'

'He's not doing anything,' I pointed out. 'Just looking round. I expect he's new to the area.'

'Mmm.' She was still worrying. 'I don't like people who know nothing about horses hanging round. He might try and feed them something horrible.'

'Why should he?' I pushed away the scornful look of yesterday. 'He's got nothing against us.'

I turned back to the yard to do a bit more work on Charlie's mane. He was definitely brighter, looking around him with more interest and calling to us when we came back from our ride. He hadn't minded the mane and tail washing but didn't think much of all the pulling and tugging I was forced to do to get the old burrs, tangles and general muck out.

'You're still a very good boy about it all,' I told him as he stood at the door, munching his hay and keeping an eye on this nice new world of his.

I was busy chatting and brushing when Mum came over. 'That Kevin's gone,' she announced. 'He hung round for a while after you'd gone, as if he was waiting for something, then he pushed off.'

'Kez,' I corrected her, trying not to sound as if I cared.

'I thought it was Kev, short for Kevin.' She was surprised. 'I wonder what Kez stands for?'

'Dunno.' I straightened my aching arm. 'That's what the other boys called him, definitely.'

'Is he foreign?' Mum's always intrigued by names. 'He's very dark, I noticed; could he be Mediterranean or Arabic maybe?'

'No,' I said shortly. 'His eyes are blue. Really blue.'

'Oh. Black hair and blue eyes, that's Irish usually. Did he have an accent, Fran?'

'I really didn't notice.' I was overdoing the couldn't-care-less bit, and I knew it and she knew it. 'I don't think so. He only said a few words.'

'Whatever they were, they got to you all right.'

I didn't answer and she sighed. 'Come on, tell me about it. You don't seem to have a girlfriend you can share all this sort of stuff with, so won't I do? I won't laugh, if that's what you think.'

I knew she wouldn't, but I couldn't put how I felt about Kez into words, not to anybody. 'There's nothing to tell.' I shrugged, trying to convince myself as well as her that I really didn't care. 'As you say, that lot just poke fun at anything they don't understand. I suppose this Kez hates us because he thinks we're the idle rich, owning horses.'

'Idle rich! What a wonderful expression,' Mum did her

uproarious laugh. 'Chance would be a fine thing. What makes you think he hates us at all, though, Fran? A bit of mickey-taking doesn't usually go very deep, you know.'

'It was the look he gave me.' I shuddered, I couldn't help it. 'He wasn't teasing or fooling around. He hates me all right.'

She looked worried again. 'I'll keep an eye out for him. If what you say is right we don't want him hanging round here.'

So we got on with our lives, busier than ever now, and although we sometimes saw Kez standing by the fence at the far edge of the field, he never attempted to approach us or the horses, so we just left it and forgot about him. At least Mum did. I still thought about him quite a lot.

Not for the first time I wished I had a friend in the village I could talk to, and maybe find out more about this mysterious figure who'd suddenly appeared on the scene. I didn't, though. I still hadn't really met any of the kids who were my nearest neighbours, my only contact with people of my own age being at school where most of the girls were boarders. They came from all over the place – Scotland, Cornwall, London, even one from California – but not one lived in the village.

I told them about Charlie, of course, and how he was progressing, and mentioned Kez too.

'He sounds kinda dreamy.' Kelly, from California, was a great romantic. 'So good-looking and different from all those other guys. I bet he's a prince or something, just waiting to hear that his father, who renounced him, has died and he's now king.'

'King of where?' I laughed at her.

'Oh, I don't know, some fabulous little kingdom in Europe. He probably looked real mad at you because he wants you for his queen but knows he can't marry a commoner.'

I hadn't thought of that, I must admit. Mum, for once, was the practical one and came up with the answer by talking to the local greengrocer.

'You were right, that lad's name is Kez,' she announced, a few days after Charlie had moved in. 'He's a cousin of the Whitleys. Apparently his mother, Sarah Whitley – a very pretty girl with bright blue eyes, the grocer said – ran off with a Romany years ago and Kez is the result. She died and the Whitleys let him come to them instead of an orphanage.'

So, not a European prince, but a displaced gypsy. I thought it was still romantic, and quite sad.

'No wonder he looks angry,' Mum went on. 'That crowded council house must be a far cry from the open road.'

'I thought that real Romanies knew all there was to know about horses.' I was still being carefully casual. 'So it wasn't ignorance that made him look at me like that.'

Mum shrugged. 'If he hasn't long lost his mother he'd be feeling pretty grim. I think you're over-reacting. I don't expect the look was particularly directed at you.'

But it had been. I was quite sure of that. I resolutely pushed the thought away and concentrated on nursing Charlie back to health. He was a darling to look after, patient and well behaved whatever I did. The good food and treatment worked wonders and in a couple of weeks you could really see the difference in him. The sores on his face were still healing, but his skinny body had filled out quite well and most of its cuts and grazes were gone.

One Saturday morning the early spring sunshine was sending warm, pale fingers across the yard and I decided to give the chestnut his first outing in our paddock. He was as good as gold with the headcollar, which I still padded, and had been led round the yard several times for the vet and the farrier, so he stepped out of his box in his usual quiet, good-mannered way.

We'd already turned Brontë and Woolf out without their rugs to get the benefit of the sun on their backs, and Charlie turned his lovely dark eyes to look at them. He started to perk up as soon as I led him towards the paddock gate, and Mum, who was watching, said, 'He can't believe his luck. Look how he's stepping out now.'

Indeed, his neatly trimmed hooves were almost dancing, but I made him stop and stand correctly while I undid the gate to the spring paddock. We'd had the field rolled and harrowed in the autumn and the grass was already looking wonderful. Woolf and Brontë cantered over to the fence, all agog to see what was going on. Brontë looked quite affronted, as if to say 'That's *our* grass for later on!', but Woolf whickered eagerly to welcome his new neighbour.

I led Charlie in and gently removed the headcollar. He stood for a moment, looking first at me, then at the glorious expanse of fresh green grass – and just about went mad with joy. He galloped and bucked and spun across the field, the sun sparking gold where his sleek summer coat was beginning to show. At the far end of the field he wheeled and turned, striking his legs out proudly in a beautiful extended trot, head high and tail flowing.

I felt a lump in my throat and tears prickle the back of my eyes, thinking of the contrast between this beautiful, joy-filled horse with his perfection of movement, and the beaten, sorry scrap of an animal whose eyes had almost lost hope. I turned to Mum and saw *her* eyes were all damp and shiny.

I gulped severely, it wouldn't do for us both to bawl, and said, 'I just hope I can catch the bloomin' horse again, that's all!'

'Oh, Fran,' she half sobbed, half laughed and hugged me. 'You're so practical. Don't you think he looks wonderful? Isn't it all worth it just to see him enjoying life like that?'

It was, of course.

'Mmm,' I said. 'He's a long way from looking wonderful but we're on our way, I think. He can have a couple of hours out today while it's warm and we'll build it up gradually.'

Apart from Charlie reaping the benefits of grazing the spring grass, this was also an ideal way of introducing the three horses outdoors. I wasn't really worried they'd fight, but there's sometimes the odd skirmish while they're working out the pecking order. I was pretty sure that Brontë would be herd leader – she's bossy by nature and both Woolf and Charlie are softies.

Mum and I stayed and watched Charlie for a while. Once he'd got over the heady joy of being free, untrammelled by a horrible tether, the first thing he did was have a good roll, back squirming and hooves waving ecstatically. He then got up, shook vigorously, touched noses with Woolf across the fence and settled down to some serious grazing. We left him to it until it was time for our afternoon ride.

I brought the other two horses into the yard first, thinking if Charlie was going to be any trouble, he'd be less likely to try and avoid coming in if his friends were already there. In fact, as with everything, he was a lamb. I walked to the gate, called his name, and he trotted straight over. I rewarded him with titbits, not something I usually do, but he really was being specially good.

I thought he looked lonely when we left on our ride but when Mum said, 'Poor Charlie, I do feel mean leaving him,' I told her not to be silly.

She got quite cross and said I was getting above myself, and that just because I was in charge of Charlie, it didn't mean I could boss her around too. I said she *needed* someone to tell her what to do, and then we had one of our short, sharp arguments, which ended with

Mum galloping off on Woolf, leaving me and little Brontë pottering away in the rear.

When we reached the top of the hill they'd disappeared and I had a panic attack that she'd fallen off, been run away with or had a million other accidents. Rising rapidly to Brontë's somewhat bumpy trot, I was peering anxiously around when she and Woolf suddenly leapt out from behind a bush. Mum tweaked my mare's tail, making her buck like mad, then cantered past us, roaring with laughter. We gave chase, of course, but Brontë's little legs are no match for Woolf's long and elegant stride, and Mum kept galloping along directly in front of us so we got mouthfuls of mud and stones.

I told you she was a loony. Woolf's exactly the same and they make a terrifying pair. It was good fun, though, and we returned at a nice cooling walk to our yard, still laughing, and friends again. Charlie called out as soon as he heard us and Woolf whinnied back immediately. I thought gladly what good friends these two were going to be, and began the tea-time chores with a real glow of happiness in me.

The next few weeks went to plan. Charlie improved daily, and as the weather got better too, we turned them all out in the spring paddock, happy in the knowledge they could use the stout, three-sided shelter if rain, wind or heat made them uncomfortable.

They looked wonderful out there in the field together. Brontë's pretty little head and pert pony shape were offset by Woolf's darkly dramatic good looks, and now Charlie in the burnished copper of his summer coat looked every bit as handsome. They got on well too, the two geldings staying together while the more independent grey mare liked to graze alone, keeping a strict eye on 'the boys' and making sure they stayed in line.

Ben had been trimming Charlie's feet regularly and the

cracks were growing out fast, with beautifully healthy new hoof growth above them. He said next time he called he'd put some shoes on so we could start riding the chestnut horse.

'Bet you're dying to try him out,' he said to me. 'You've brought him on an absolute treat, about time he started repaying you.'

I actually wasn't that fussy about the riding bit, and although I wouldn't mind Ben knowing that, I wouldn't want to look a wimp in front of his new apprentice. Steve was sixteen and quite good looking in a ferrety way, I suppose, but I didn't like him. So I lied enthusiastically.

'Mmm. Mum thinks Charlie will make a show jumper from his action. Can't wait to ride him.'

'I'll take him round the field for you,' Steve offered grandly. 'Put some poles up and I'll see if he can jump.'

'I'd rather not till he's shod,' I said quickly. 'I don't want to undo all the hard work we've put in on his feet. Anyway we've been waiting for him to fill out properly before we buy a saddle.'

'Just shove Woolf's on him. It won't hurt.' Steve was starting to get on my nerves and I was glad when Ben clouted his shoulder and said, 'Leave it, pushy. Fran will do the riding when she's ready. See you next week then, give your mum my love and tell her I'm sorry I missed her.'

'Will do.' I waved them out of the yard and gave Charlie a hug for standing like an angel as usual. He had such perfect stable manners and a wonderful temperament when it came to being handled, I was beginning to worry just what the flaw was in this seemingly perfect horse. It sounds silly, but I'd decided he was probably a maniac under saddle, and like I say, I love to ride but only when I know I'm the one in control. Woolf absolutely terrified me, he was so unpredictable and scatty, and whereas Mum just laughed and ignored him when he threw a tantrum, I froze with fear.

The big bay, like Charlie, was no problem to handle, just a bit ticklish to groom sometimes, but once you got on his back it was a different story. The thought that my sweet, gentle Charlie might turn out to be just the same filled me with dread, though I hadn't actually admitted as much to Mum yet. The trouble was, if he was going to be too hot for me to ride, there wasn't much point in keeping him. The plan at present was that Mum and Woolf would keep their crazy partnership, and as Brontë was beginnning to show her age and was already on the small side for me, she'd take a well deserved semi-retirement and Charlie would be my 'first' horse. All very well as long as I could cope with him!

FOUR

I STOOD BACK and took a good look at the chestnut horse. He really had turned out to be a beauty. The scars from the old cuts were barely visible now – even his badly marked face had healed – and the coat was shining with health. He was well made with a deep chest, good length of back, and the broad, muscular loins which provide a perfect foundation for the muscles used in jumping. The quarters needed building up with some steady work, but his tendons were strong, dropping straight to the fetlock.

With his beautiful head, kind eyes and sprung ribcage he presented the ideal picture of a well bred, high spirited horse – and my heart sank. Don't get me wrong, I didn't want a donkey, but I knew I wasn't up to a handful like Woolf. Mum drove in and caught me staring at him.

'Hi-ya. You look as though all the worries in the world have just landed on you. What's the matter? Ben not pleased with Charlie's feet?'

'He says they're really improving. That vitamin supplement is working wonders.'

'Good-oh.' She patted Charlie's nicely rounded rump and said, 'So what's up?'

It was no good pretending. She can always see right through me. 'I'm a bit nervous about riding him. Steve said he'd take him round the jumps, and if I'd liked the boy better I'd have said yes.'

'Oh?' she ran her fingers through her hair, forgetting it was in a bun. 'Damn, now see what I've done. You don't need Steve. I'll try Charlie out first if you like.'

'Oh no.' I was definite on that point. 'He's my pigeon. Anyway if he is batty you'll love him. And he's not for you to ride – you've got your ideal maniac in Woolf.'

'Woolf is a perfectly good horse, he just has a few...

30

er...eccentricities.' She was trying to go all dignified.

'Oh yeah,' I said drily. 'Like bombing off, stopping dead, shying at shadows, jumping puddles, squealing at sheep...'

'OK, OK,' she waved her hand airily. 'I take your point. But just because *he's* like that doesn't mean Charlie will be, you know. If I was stricter about schooling and hadn't let Woolf develop these little habits he'd probably be...well...normal.'

'Maybe.' I wasn't convinced. Better perhaps, but normal never! 'The trouble is it's a lot of money investing in new tack and if I can't manage Charlie...'

'You old pessimist.' I got another hug. 'Always worrying about something. We'll get the tack, try him gently, give him time to settle down to working again, and if you don't like him we'll sell him *with* the tack. All right?'

'It's not a question of me not liking him.' I felt the irritating tears start to prickle again. 'I do, but...'

'Stop fretting then. He might not even be broken... have you thought of that?'

'Oh, but he is.' I grinned suddenly. 'I'm not quite as wet as I sound. I've ridden him across the field and he knows what leg aids are, certainly.'

'Yah!' Mum made a face at me. 'You're not wet at all, you demon. Ride him back to the paddock now, then.'

I climbed on the yard fence and slid gently onto Charlie's sun-warmed back. He was only in a headcollar of course, so I guided him with my legs to the gate and trotted him across to where the other two were grazing. I slid off, took off the headcollar, and watched him have a funny five minutes with his friend Woolf, the pair of them bucking and kicking and skipping like spring lambs.

Mum was laughing her head off. 'Look at that! Charlie is definitely the perfect gentleman. There was nothing to stop him belting off like that with you aboard, but he waited till you were safely on the ground.'

31

'True.' I felt happier immediately and, shielding my eyes from the sun, squinted across the field. 'They're both rolling now...look and...oh!'

'What is it?' She tried to follow my gaze.

'There's someone watching,' I said slowly. 'Right over there by the road fence.'

She put on sunglasses and said immediately, 'It's that gypsy boy, isn't it? What's his name again?'

'Kez,' I sighed 'I wonder how long he's been there.'

'I've a good mind to chase him off,' Mum said worriedly.

'Why? He can't do anything from there. The horses aren't even in that field any more, and he hasn't shown any sign of coming onto our land to touch them or anything.'

'It's very odd.' Mum still screwed her eyes up behind the glasses. 'I just don't like people hanging round here.'

'Mmm, well he's going again.' I'd been watching the lean figure. 'He'll get fed up with it eventually. We're hardly the most exciting family in the world to spy on.'

'You don't know,' Mum said darkly. 'It's times like this we could do with a man about the place.'

'Perhaps farmer Weldon would lend us a scarecrow,' I suggested. 'Though a cardboard cutout would look more effective.'

'And so cheap to keep.' She bashed me in her usual friendly way.

'And he wouldn't answer back.' I laughed at her. 'Or make you tidy up the place.'

'Perfect.' She sighed theatrically and we wandered back to the house giggling again.

The next day the saddler arrived to measure me and Charlie. Mum wasn't letting the grass grow under her feet. We settled for a comfortable secondhand GP saddle which fitted Charlie to perfection and felt good to me, too. A simple English leather bridle with a plain jointed snaffle and a set of plaited reins completed the buying. We were quite well off for boots and rugs and all the other para-phernalia and I decided not even to think about things like dropped nosebands and martingales.

'I'm just going to assume he's the perfect gentleman, as you said,' I told Mum. 'So gadgets won't be necessary.'

"Course not,' she agreed. 'He's going to be a doddle.'

The saddler wanted to put a little extra stuffing in the sadle panels so he arranged to deliver it the following Friday, when Charlie was going to be fitted with his shoes. That meant a week tomorrow was 'C' day – the day I finally rode out on my beautiful chestnut Charlie. I was exhilarated and terrified at the same time, most of me putting my trust in the gentle horse, but just a little bit, the cowardly bit, shaking at the knees at the very thought.

The other vision that added to the trembling was the one where I imagined us riding out of the yard and coming face to face with the scornful, blue-eyed gaze of the dark-haired gypsy, Kez.

And of course when 'C' day did arrive, we rode out onto the road and there he was walking towards us! I was feeling pretty precarious perched on my new saddle on my new horse. I've admitted I'm not that brave and I was just waiting for the perfect Charlie to be less than perfect and throw me off. The last thing I needed was another withering look from Kez, so I turned my head away quickly and hoped the chestnut horse wouldn't notice that my knees were now trembling more than ever.

I usually wait for Mum when it's her turn to shut the gate, because Woolf is still silly about standing properly, but I was so keen to get away from the hatred I knew would be on Kez's face I kept Charlie going at a brisk walk. Poor Mum, leaning down to latch the gate, found herself fighting a panic-stricken Woolf, who was quite sure his friend was leaving him for ever. The batty horse danced and fidgeted and pulled back and Mum nearly fell off trying to bring him back to the gate. She managed eventually and caught me up, slightly out of breath and understandably snappy.

'What are you doing, bombing off like that?' she demanded. 'Is Charlie playing you up?'

'No,' I admitted, shamefaced. 'I wanted to keep going so I wouldn't have to speak to Kez.'

'Ye gods, you're paranoid about that boy.' She rubbed her arm, sore from Woolf's pulling. 'He's gone again now and I *wanted* to speak to him, to find out just why he keeps hanging round us. I suppose you're going to tell me he looks as though he hates us more than ever?'

'I don't know.' I was starting to relax. Charlie was walking beautifully along the lane and my panic attack now seemed as ridiculous as Woolf's. 'I didn't look at him today.'

'Honestly!' she was quite cross. 'You are the limit, Fran. This bloomin' horse has yanked my arms out of their sockets.'

'*My* horse is behaving perfectly,' I said smugly and irritatingly.

'Well, hooray for you.' I wasn't improving her temper. 'You didn't really think I'd let you out on the road if he wasn't safe, did you? I got the local BHS instructor to check him out first. *She* says he's bomb-proof, too, but after what you just did to me, I almost hope there's something that will make him misbehave.'

But there wasn't. Charlie walked briskly along the lane, totally ignoring a tractor and went beautifully into working trot as soon as I asked.

Woolf, of course, rolled his eyes and shied at the tractor even though he'd seen it before, and when Charlie trotted, Woolf did his naughty impression of a rocking horse, cantering on the spot and pulling like a train. Mum groaned and gritted her teeth, but by the time we reached the wide open space of the common she had him back under control. By then I was really enjoying myself.

Charlie was even better behaved than Brontë and so much more comfortable. His cadence was perfect, and each transition was executed perfectly, flowing easily from trot into canter and down again. We rode along a narrow, twisting path and I asked for leg change on each bend. He seemed a little unbalanced a couple of times but that was probably because he needed some muscle building work to bring him back to top form.

I loved him more than ever and felt so confident on him I even suggested we popped them over a couple of small jumps we'd made. Mum was impressed and forgot to be annoyed with me any more.

'You really like him, don't you?' She grinned in her usual exuberant way.

'I certainly do.' I hugged Charlie's slightly damp neck and we headed for home at a cooling-down pace.

I could tell the horse had enjoyed the outing as much as I had and felt so happy I sang all the way back. I didn't even mind when Mum joined in in her own unmusical way. What she lacks in tune-holding she makes up for in volume. I usually cringe and hope I won't meet anyone I know, but that day I carried on singing with her and even found myself hoping we'd see Kez again. I felt so confident I knew I could take him on, vicious stare and all. He'd vanished though, and all our singing did was frighten a couple of cows.

We rode out nearly every day after that, and as Charlie got fitter and fitter it just got better and better. Kez seemed to have given up hanging round the place and my life was so full and so happy I almost stopped worrying about him.

Then one day, after we'd done a brisk circuit of the common and were cantering along a bridlepath that skirts a big wheat field, something terrible happened. I was leading – we felt it would teach Woolf to stop pulling all the time if he got used to being following file sometimes – and Charlie was showing off his beautiful controlled canter. He and I resolutely ignored the snorts and frustrated huffing of Woolf as he battled with Mum in the hope of being allowed to pass us, and gradually it seemed she was winning.

I glanced over my shoulder and saw she'd managed to keep him a good length off our tail, and although he was still rolling his wicked eyes, he'd at least dropped his nose and stopped fighting the bit. Mum was grinning away, enjoying his naughtiness as she always did, when suddenly disaster struck. A young rabbit shot out from amongst the wheat just ahead of the big bay. Shelley and Sam, loping happily along in the rear, spotted it and set up a terrific barking. Woolf, who's heard that sound a thousand times and seen hundreds of rabbits in his life, decided it was the most frightening situation he'd ever known, and shied violently sideways.

Mum's so used to him she hardly budged out of the saddle, but before she had a chance to straighten him up and get him back on the track, the silly horse slipped somehow and went down, legs thrashing wildly among the green shoots of wheat. This time Mum's staying-aboard powers were her worst enemy: instead of being thrown clear she was trapped underneath the struggling Woolf, her right leg taking the brunt of his weight. It seemed like a scene filmed in slow motion though in reality there were only a few seconds of slip-slip-struggle-chaos, then Woolf was on his feet again, reins and stirrup leathers flapping.

But my mum was lying unconscious on the bruised and flattened field, her right leg bent at a sickening angle and her face as white as the clouds scudding above us. The dogs had gone steaming after the rabbit, and

36

although I stopped Charlie immediately and spun him round, I wasn't quick enough to catch Woolf's looping reins and the bay, in a blind panic, tore straight by and disappeared from sight.

I threw myself off my horse and knelt beside my mother. She lay very still and quiet, and for a dreadful, dreadful moment I thought she wasn't breathing. I laid my head on her chest, heard her strong, regular heartbeat, and tried to force down the panic that had risen in my throat. Charlie and I were alone in the field and at least a mile from any main road, with an injured, possibly a very badly injured, person. Obviously we had to get help, but to leave her there, crushed into the spiky blades of wheat without anyone to help or comfort her when she came round, didn't bear thinking of.

I tried to think; in desperation, I even considered sending Charlie off with some kind of message on his saddle, but that sort of thing only works in fiction. In real life the horse would either get knocked down by a lorry, or it would simply belt off home and wait all forlornly to be let in, not realising it was supposed to be on a rescue mission.

The dogs were no good either. They'd come back, all shamefaced and rabbitless (they never do catch anything), and I knew trying to make them leave us was hopeless too. Shelley whimpered and licked Mum's face, but she still didn't stir and I felt sick and helpless and frightened. I had to leave her; I had to go and get help – and then Charlie whickered suddenly and I held my breath. I could hear hoof beats, a steady rhythmic trotting, somewhere nearby.

I called out: 'Help! Please! There's been an accident.'

I looked wildly up the track we'd just come along, then realised the sound was coming from behind me, and turned quickly, hoping against hope the rider had heard my cry. The hoofbeat pattern changed into the three-time pounding of canter and I realised thankfully it was getting louder, coming towards us, not heading away. The bridle-path curves away at that point, winding around the edge of the big field, and although it could only have been minutes, it seemed an age before horse and rider appeared. The sun was behind them and for an instant I thought we were being rescued by a knight on a fiery black charger. The sun gilded the knight's dark hair with a golden halo and he sat lightly astride his prancing steed, easily controlling the fluid, fast-moving pace.

Charlie snorted and shook his mane in recognition, breaking the spell, and as they came out of the sun I saw the horse wasn't black, but dark bay, the rider not a knight but the Romany, Kez. I gasped and stammered something and he slid off Woolf's back and knelt swiftly at Mum's side.

'Don't move her. Just make sure her airway stays clear and cover her with something.' He vaulted onto Woolf's back and wheeled him sharply, hands and heels light but insistent.

The big bay thundered back down the track leading to the road, and I fumbled to undo my jacket with fingers that would not stop trembling. I dropped Charlie's reins tugging off my jumper but he stayed right where he was, looking down, as I gently covered Mum's small, still form with the clothes. I listened to her heart again and tried to check her pulse. Her skin felt quite cold and when a whimpering Shelley crept close and snuggled against her side I didn't stop him. Sam was too big – he might tread on her injured leg – so I kept him next to me and, holding Mum's hand, tried to get some warmth from him. It was a lovely spring day, but despite the sun the wind was chill, and in just a tee-shirt and jods I was soon shivering with cold as well as shock.

The young green wheat swayed and sighed in the

38

breeze and somewhere a bird was singing, but there was no human sound. No one else, it seemed, was using the bridlepath. I squeezed Mum's hand and silently thanked the miraculous appearance of Kez. I knew he'd have to ride Woolf the mile or so down the track, then at least another mile to the nearest farmhouse where there'd be a phone. I didn't dare think how long it would all take, couldn't face the thought that Kez might have trouble with the unpredictable bay horse or find no one at the farm, or that the ambulance might not be able to make it along the bumpy field edge.

I checked Mum's breathing for the hundredth time and tried to ignore the tears that were trickling down my face. Sam leaned forward and licked my chin helpfully, then growled low in his throat and turned his head towards the bend in the track.

'What is it? Can you hear something?' I wiped the back of the hand that wasn't holding Mum's across my face and listened.

Charlie had been quietly cropping the grass nearby but he raised his head and whinnied. A distant, but rapidly approaching, neighing sounded in reply and minutes later Woolf came cantering into sight.

Behind him was the wonderfully comforting sight of an ambulance, bucking and dipping across the ruts, but almost, almost at my mother's side. The two paramedics jumped out immediately and started examining her. They said her leg was definitely broken, she had concussion and probably other injuries, but they had to risk moving her so that she could get hospital treatment as quickly as possible. They turned the ambulance to face back towards the road and in an amazingly short time had lifted her, strapped onto a stretcher, into its interior, and were bumping, as gently as they could, away from us.

FIVE

Kez held both horses' reins while I struggled cold arms into my sweater and jacket. He'd shoved Shelley firmly under one arm to stop him running after the ambulance, and his brilliant blue eyes looked at me with concern.

'Will you be able to ride?' His voice was softer, the bitter edge I remembered completely missing.

I nodded. 'I think so. I'm just a bit...cold and shaky.'

He immediately handed me Shelley, whipped off his own jacket and told me to put it on. Then he tapped the little terrier on the nose and said, 'We'll walk a bit till your arms and legs come back to life and this little horror decides to stay put.'

I wanted to get home, but he was right about the arms and legs. There was no way I could even climb aboard Charlie the state they were in, so we started walking, leading the horses and encouraging Shelley to stay at Sam's side. Kez's jacket was thick and warm and smelled...I don't know...comfortingly masculine. He kept Woolf on his right and walked next to me, talking quietly. Gradually the warmth returned to my frozen limbs and the frightening sense of unreality faded.

'That's better.' Kez was smiling and I blinked at the transformation it worked on his lean face. If I'd thought he was good-looking the first time I saw him, he was like a Greek god with those beautiful white teeth and warmth in his blue eyes.

Despite my overwhelming concern for my mum I was suddenly aware what a sight I must be, face all tear-stained, hair damp and flat under my riding hat and body swamped under the bulk of Kez's coat. I sniffed unbeautifully and turned away.

'I'm OK to ride now,' I said brusquely. 'And I need to get home quickly. I'll have to see to all the animals before I can get to Mum in hospital.'

He gave me a swift, professional leg-up onto Charlie's back and swung himself easily aboard the lofty Woolf.

'And we thought you knew nothing about horses.' Despite my embarrassment at myself I grinned at the thought, and he flashed that wonderful, warm smile again.

'What made you think that?'

'I don't know.' I lowered my eyes and tried to block out the memory of that first, scathing look.

I could feel his eyes on me. 'Come on, Fran. You've had a hell of a shock. Talk to me. Tell me why you thought that of me. It'll help you get back to normal.'

'Whatever normal is.' I hesitated. The village boys must have told him my name, he'd called me Fran, so I thought he wouldn't mind me using his.

'Kez, do you think...do you think she'll be all right?'

'She's in the right hands. Concussion always looks terrifying but once they get her into hospital and bring her round, she'll be fine. Her hat saved her from any major head injury, and broken legs do mend, you know.'

'Mmm.' I'd closed my eyes, grateful I didn't have to concentrate too much on riding the beautifully behaved Charlie. Woolf was trying to jog as usual but Kez's light touch brought him back to walk almost immediately.

'Behave yourself, horse.' His voice was still gentle. 'And listen, Fran's going to tell us what she thought I was doing hanging round your field all these weeks if I don't like horses. And she's going to say why she always looks at me as if I'm the bogey man. Come along, Fran, we want to know.'

I managed a smile and, with an effort, made myself answer him. He was right, it was better to talk than think about Mum. 'It was the first day I saw you,' I blurted in a rush. 'Mum had just done a rescue act on Charlie and I was leading him home because he wouldn't go in the trailer. He still won't; it's the only thing I can't get him to do. Anyway, I walked past you, I don't suppose you remember...'

'I remember.' His face was expressionless.

'Yes. Well, you made the others let me pass and when I tried to thank you, you looked at me...' I closed my eyes again. '...you looked at me as if you hated me, really despised me.'

My tears were obviously just lurking below the surface, despite trying not to think about Mum's accident, and one rolled fatly down my cheek. Kez held Woolf easily in one hand and wiped it away with the other.

'Sorry.' I was embarrassed. 'We thought, you see, that you resented us for being 'horsey' people, thinking our type were over-privileged or something.'

'I gave you that look,' he said quietly, 'because I was truly disgusted that you could half-starve and ill-treat your horse. I didn't know you'd just rescued Charlie. Jake told me you'd always had your own pony and I thought you'd let the poor thing get into that state yourself.'

'Is that why you kept hanging round our paddock?'

'Yes. I decided to tell you some home truths about the way you treated your animals. I couldn't understand at first why Woolf here and the little grey were in such good shape. Then you turned Charlie out and I saw the transformation you'd made. I was going to congratulate you the other day when you both rode out, but you made it clear you didn't want to see me.'

'Only because I didn't understand why you seemed to hate us. You should have come to the house.' I smiled fully at him, but it was his turn to look away.

'My kind aren't always welcome,' he muttered, and swayed slightly as Woolf put in one of his enormous shies.

42

'You ride him so well.' My admiration was genuine but I also wanted to change the subject as it seemed to upset him.

'He's a horror.' His voice was immediately more cheerful. 'Your mum's an excellent rider but she shouldn't let him get away with his tricks.'

'She didn't have a chance today,' I said defensively. 'Woolf slipped somehow and actually went down.'

'He really is a head case, I can see that,' he glanced at me, concern in his blue eyes. 'You're upset again, Fran.'

'I'm...it's probably my fault,' I burst out. 'We were making Woolf follow, you see, and Mum had been really battling to get him under control, then there was this rabbit...'

'Fran, it wasn't your fault.' I would never have believed from his tough exterior that he could be so gentle. 'It was just one of those things. Woolf's a horse of little brain and what he's got seems to be in sideways. You and your mum were doing everything right. The horse just fell, so stop blaming yourself.'

'But if you hadn't come along...' I was close to tears again.

'Well, I did,' he said cheerfully. 'There I was, knee deep in a ditch, when I heard the big lad thundering down the track. I knew my herb gathering would come in useful one day and I was right.'

'*Herb* gathering?' I looked sceptical. 'You mean wild flowers and stuff?'

'Don't you start...I get enough mickey-taking from Jake and his mates,' he laughed, showing his white teeth. 'You can imagine the sort of comments they come up with whenI go back with bunches of meadowsweet or comfrey.'

He was trying to stop me worrying, and the picture he conjured up of the gang's reaction was funny enough to make me relax into a smile. I was also curious.

'What do you use those for?'

'The leaves of meadowsweet are good for stomach disorders. They contain the same acid as aspirin but don't have any of its side-effects. Comfrey's a useful external healing plant. I make poultices from it.'

I gazed at him with new respect. 'You really do know. Where did you learn all this?'

'From my gran, the one on Dad's side.' I thought he was going to go all prickly again, but he tilted his chin almost defiantly. 'She was a gypsy, a full-blooded Romany, and she knew every plant and every remedy that could be made from it.'

'And she taught you. Did she teach you to ride like that too?'

'No, that was my dad. My mother used to say he was born on a horse, he looked so much a part of one when he rode. I've seen him take a wild colt and turn him into a trusting, perfectly behaved working horse in no time at all. He never ever hurried an animal, but he knew just how to bring out the best in one.'

'And you're the same.' I'd noticed how much calmer Woolf was, even in the short time Kez had been riding him.

'Wish I was.' His eyes were sad and far away. 'I'd like to have something of his and that would be...' He shook himself, literally, and the bay horse flicked his ears. 'Anyway, we're nearly at your home...what's the plan? How can I help?'

'You've done so much already.' The panic I'd been pushing down threatened to rise again. 'But I would appreciate it if you could help me with the animals. I've got to get to the hospital, of course, but I have to feed everyone and put them away for the night.'

'Just show me who goes where and who gets what and I'll do it.' He sounded confident and in control, and I was grateful. 'You call someone to go with you and I'll get everything straight while you're there.'

I hadn't thought of phoning anyone. It's just Mum and me. We don't have anyone else close to us.

'I can't think who to tell.' I was being very inept and girlie. 'I'll just get a taxi.'

'What about your dad? Steady, Woolf.' The daft horse was dancing sideways at a threatening paper bag.

'He and his second wife are on holiday. I got a card from them yesterday. They're in Arizona.'

'My cousin Jake told me it was just you and your mother living here. But don't you have a gran or grand-dad?' Kez was still speaking very gently.

'Not nearby.' I could only think of my mum, lying there in the hospital.

Kez seemed to understand. 'The main thing is to get you there to be with her. Just give me the low-down on feeding time at the Harper Zoo and get going.'

There seemed to be so many details, but he made brief notes as I showed him round the store room, the hen house and the pigsty.

He looked gravely over the sty wall and said solemnly 'One pig,' and wrote down what he got for tea.

I felt a sudden mad urge to giggle at that and Kez pretended to raise a shocked eyebrow.

The taxi arrived and I dashed off in a last-minute flurry of 'Don't forget to lock the hens up,' and 'They wander all over the place, you'll have to count them,' and 'Make sure Pinter doesn't pinch Ayckbourn's food'.

The taxi driver looked bemused at that one and Kez scratched his head too. 'Which one's which?'

I jumped into the cab and wound down the window. 'Pinter's black.'

'Got it.' The car moved off and he yelled, 'Don't worry. Everything'll be fine. I'll stay here till you phone.'

'Get yourself some tea then, there's plenty...' but we'd driven out of the gate and I couldn't see him any more.

SIX

I'D TOLD THE cabby it was an urgent run to the hospital and he did the trip in superquick time. I saw him glance in the mirror at me once or twice as I sat clutching a bag with Mum's slippers and nightclothes in it. In the rush I hadn't been able to find a sponge bag, and her tooth-brush and flannel were rolled in a polythene carrier. I was worrying about that and worrying about Kez finding everything, especially Byron who wandered off all over the place. By doing a lot of minor fretting I wouldn't allow myself to think about the major worry of just how badly hurt my mother was. The driver was nice; he dropped me off right outside the main door and wouldn't take a tip.

'You keep it love. I'm sure your mum'll be OK and your boyfriend will soon sort out that Pinter bloke.'

I would have giggled if I hadn't felt so sick. I thanked him and took his telephone number for when I was ready to go home. I walked into the hospital and I swear people on the far side of the waiting room could hear my heart thumping.

'Mrs Harper?' The receptionist glanced through her notes. 'You're her daughter? Is your dad or another relative with you?'

I shook my head.

'Take a seat, please, Fran, and I'll get someone to find out how Mum is and come and tell you.'

'She's not dead then,' I thought and wanted to burst into tears.

I know it sounds melodramatic but that was the big fear I'd been fighting. I waited for a while, then a nurse came over and took me along a shiny echoing corridor to another chair outside another room. I asked to see Mum and was told that she was still unconscious and that the doctor would come and see me. I waited again, feeling numb. "Still unconscious" sounded dreadful. I was holding the bag that held her things so tightly my fingers had gone all stiff. It's strange, the rest of that evening is blurred and fuzzy, but I can still flex my hands and remember how they felt.

I do know the hospital arranged for me to stay overnight in a room near Mum, and someone phoned my Aunt Eleanor so that she'd come over the next day. I ate something, I don't know what, and I think I drank some tea and some milk. I know I called my home number and Kez took ages to answer.

'That you, Fran?' He sounded breathless. 'Sorry, I was catching the bantam.'

'Are you having problems?' I tried to stop thinking about Mum, lying so still in the white bed with tubes and drips and bleeping things around her.

'Not a bit. I got round the Pinter problem by feeding them in separate rooms. Clever, eh? Oh, and Shelley broke the cat-flap but I've mended it. And I took the food for Willow, the outdoor-living-cat, to the barn. You did say I could make myself some tea?'

'Yes. Please do.' I felt odd and remote.

'I please did. Beans and cheese on toast.'

'Good. Kez, I have to ask you another favour.'

'Ask away. I'm enjoying it.'

I knew he meant it. 'I'm going to have to stay here tonight in case Mum comes round. You couldn't possibly do the morning feeds as well?'

'Spend the night here, you mean?' He sounded doubtful.

'Well, if you don't want to do that...' I began.

'It's not I don't want to. I'd be glad to, and Jake's family won't give a hoot. It's just...your mum doesn't know I'm here in your house and she might not be too happy about me staying overnight.'

'Don't be silly.' I brushed a tired hand across my face. 'She'll be totally grateful.'

'OK. Don't give the place another thought. You concentrate on your mum. She's going to be fine, you'll see.'

It was only when Mum was home and that dreadful day was behind us that I realised it was Kez who got me through it.

The next morning, thankfully she regained consciousness and her first thought was for me. 'Who's looking after you, darling?'

I cried and cuddled the bits of her without needles when she spoke first, but I was soon in control again.

'The hospital called Aunt Eleanor and she's coming over today.'

Mum wrinkled her nose a bit. Eleanor's her sister, but she's a bit of a fusspot and they drive each other mad.

'I know,' I said. 'Kez and I could manage perfectly well on our own...'

'Kez?' One side of her face was swollen, giving her an eccentrically lopsided look. 'How come he's involved? Has he been hanging round the house again? He...'

I butted in swiftly and gave her the whole story of the rescue, the way Kez had got me home, and organised my trip to hospital *and* done all the chores.

'How absolutely amazing,' she blinked her eyes, one brown and one black and blue. 'What on earth was he doing on that bridlepath?'

I told her about the herbs and their healing powers and she even managed a little smile. 'Tell him to get cracking with the comfrey, then. I'm going to need at least a ton of it.'

She's so brilliant. Not one word about the wisdom of trusting Kez to stay in our house. Unlike her sister. Aunt Eleanor, though genuinely concerned about the accident, was decidedly put out about the way I'd handled it.

'Gypsies galloping about on your horses and poking

48

and prying in your cupboards.' She waved her hands about and patted her neat hair. 'At least you won't need him any more, Fran. I'll get the house straight and cook your meals for a couple of weeks till your mother's capable.'

'I honestly don't need you to.' No wonder her name hadn't sprung to mind when I wanted someone. 'I can manage as long as Kez helps with the animals.'

'Don't be silly, dear. We don't want a boy like that around.'

'That boy like that,' I spluttered incoherently, 'probably saved Mum's life!'

'Mmm.' She wasn't convinced. 'He acted very quickly I'll give him that, but...'

I took a deep breath and controlled myself. 'Look, Aunty, it's very kind of you to come all this way but I'll be perfectly all right till Mum comes home.'

'My dear child,' (Don't you just hate it when adults call you that?) 'if I don't stay here and look after you, you'll be taken into care. You're far too young to be left on your own.'

I was shocked. 'I'm nearly fifteen.'

'Still well under age.' She kissed me, putting lipstick all over my cheek, and drove me home.

There everything was in perfect order. Kez had fed and watered and mucked out all the animals, and even done all the washing up. I left my aunt tut-tutting over the state of our cupboards and went to find him. He was shovelling up the droppings in the paddock.

'You don't have to do that.' I felt suddenly shy of him.

'You do it every day, I know. How's your mum?'

I told him the good news, that her brain and personality were intact and the bad, that her body was pretty battered.

'Does she know I'm here?'

'Yes, and like I said, she's very, very grateful.' I told him what she'd said about the comfrey and he relaxed

49

enough to laugh. I felt my knees go all wobbly and told myself I must still be suffering from shock. I was very aware that my hair needed washing and I was still dressed in yesterday's grotty old jods and sweater.

To hide my embarrassment I gabbled, 'Um. My aunt's here. She's Mum's sister but she's not...'

He was very quick. 'Not so keen on my being here. I'll get out of the way then.' He started wheeling the barrow back to the yard.

'Oh, please don't.' I put my hand on his arm and felt a distinct tingle. 'Mum's told her you're to stay if you want to. Do you want to?'

His face was dark and hard again. 'If you like.'

'I do like.' I tried to lighten the tone. 'I can't manage the Harper Zoo without you, though I can certainly do without Aunt Eleanor.'

'You can't. You're not allowed to stay on your own under sixteen. Look at me. I'm stuck with my cousins. It's there or a children's home. At least you've got your mum back in a few weeks.'

There was real bitterness in his voice and Charlie wandered over and whickered softly, as if concerned. I threw my arms round the horse and buried my face in his warm, sweet-smelling neck.

'I thought...I thought for a while she wouldn't *be* coming home.' My voice was muffled in horse hair. 'You know all about that, don't you Kez?'

He ran his hand through Charlie's mane and touched my fingers briefly. 'Yes. I know. My mother died last winter. You look after yours, Fran. You only get the one.' He pulled his hand away abruptly and took himself and the barrow off.

I cried into Charlie's mane a while longer, some of it for Mum, some for me and a big, big part for Kez.

Charlie was lovely. He stood very still, and nudged me

50

gently with his nose as if he understood what it was all about. I felt a hundred times better once I'd stopped bawling and mopped my face. I pretended to check the patient horse over in case anyone was wondering why I was hanging round him like that, but in fact the anyone I had in mind had disappeared, barrow and all.

A shower and a change of clothes did me good too, and when I finally tracked Kez down to the little copse where Logic spends his day rooting about, I was feeling almost human.

He was scratching the pig behind the ears and he looked up quickly as I approached.

'Hi-ya.' I'd been scared he'd pushed off now he knew my redoubtable aunt was here.

'Your hair looks nice.' He carried on scratching and Logic grunted in ecstasy.

'You've got a friend for life there.' I felt shy about the hair. I didn't want him to think I'd washed it because of him, but I did want to get back to the easy, friendly way we'd had before.

'He's a nice chap. I've never met a *balo* before. That's Romany for pig. I know everyone must ask this, but why's he called Logic?'

I grinned. 'It's a typical Mum versus me thing. I got home from school one day and found her scrubbing away at the old pigsty we were supposed to turn into a goat pen. When I asked her why she was cleaning it up she wouldn't look me in the eye. It's always a giveaway, that.'

'Giveaway?' His dark face was still hard but the blue eyes had lost their wary look.

'That she's done something reckless. Mum acts first, thinks second. That day she'd been to market and there'd been a livestock sale. The piglets had all been sold except for a little runty one. He was frightened and squealing his head off, she said, and she didn't like the look of the

51

owner, so she bought him. I went mad.'

'Why? What's wrong with having a pig? You already had the sty to keep him in.'

'Yes, but that was going to be converted for a goat when we got round to it. I couldn't believe Mum had ruined the plan by lumbering us with a pig of all things.'

Kez looked sternly at me. 'Just because you wanted a goat and your mum preferred a pig shouldn't make you so mad at her.'

'She didn't *prefer* a pig. She just waded in and did one of her instant rescue acts. It was such a crazy thing to do, and I ranted and raved and said there was absolutely no logic in vegetarians owning a pig. A nanny goat, yes, we could use the milk, but a pig! I said it about ten times – "but there's just *no logic*"!'

Kez laughed. 'Lovely way to find a name. You never did get the nanny goat then?'

'Nah.' I pulled Logic's ears affectionately. 'And of course I couldn't possibly let this porker go now, so that's that. Still, at least the row saved him from being called Tennyson.'

He raised his eyebrows and I explained about the other battle we have over literary versus ordinary names.

'I did wonder.' He was grinning and I felt the now familiar lurch happening to my insides.

Now he had relaxed it seemed a good time to check whether he'd help while Mum was away.

His face hardened instantly, 'You know I will, but I'm not going to clash with your aunt. She's made it clear she doesn't want me around.'

'She doesn't *know* you.' The trouble was I knew he was right.

'But she knows my type...isn't that what she said? Don't look so worried, Fran, I've met this time and again since I've been here. Even Jake and his gang wouldn't use my name at first, just called me Gyppo, or worse.'

'But once they knew you...' I began, but he smiled, his eyes narrow and cold.

'No. Once I threatened to thump the next one who called me names, and once they realised I could do it, then they learned a little respect.'

I felt so sorry. He'd had such a hard life, losing his beloved dad, then his mother, and now facing hostility and prejudice from the rest of the world.

He could read my expression too. 'Don't pity me whatever you do. I'm proud of what I am.'

'So am I.' I met his eyes directly. 'And I'd be very proud if you'd be our friend. It doesn't matter about Aunt Eleanor. I want you here.'

'And your mum?' He was watching me closely.

'*And* my mum.'

The tense line of his jaw softened. 'OK, I'll give you a hand with the outside chores every day then.'

'And the exercising? I don't know when Mum will be able to ride Woolf again but he'll need to go out in the meantime.'

His face lit up again. 'I'd love to ride. Are you sure...'

'Oh, for goodness sake, I've said so.' I poked my tongue out at him and he immediately chased me back to the gate.

We were laughing and happy and I felt so much better now I knew he'd be around. I didn't even jump at my aunt's sniff of disapproval when I told her Kez and I would be taking Charlie and Woolf out. It was her misfortune to be so narrow-minded and I ought to feel sorry for her, I decided magnanimously.

She came to the door and watched us leave the yard. Woolf was being his usual idiotic self, dancing and jigging and I could see Kez was having trouble calming him. Aunt Eleanor's face was a picture as the big horse threw himself all over the yard. As soon as we were out on the road and away from her gaze, Kez relaxed visibly and was able to bring the wicked Woolf under control.

We kept the ride fairly short. Kez said the bay horse needed some steady, quiet work to wipe away the memory of yesterday's accident. As soon as we got back he hosed Woolf's legs and smoothed something into his off-fore.

'Arnica,' he said in reply to my query. 'The skin's not broken, but there's a slight swelling there. This will help the healing.'

He was very gentle with the horse but Woolf seemed to sense a certain firm authority about him and didn't play up. Kez did their feeds and put them back in the paddock with Brontë, who'd also had a thorough check-over and a small bucket. Then he helped me put the chickens away and went off with Logic's tea pail while I sorted out the cats and dogs indoors. I hoped he'd come into the kitchen, but after waiting a while I decided to go and look for him.

He'd brought the pig in from the copse and was sitting on the sty wall watching him eat.

'You're a pal,' I said lightly. 'Come and have a cup of tea.'

He smiled down at me and touched my chin. 'Stop worrying. I like doing this and I don't mind your aunt not liking me.'

'She doesn't know you,' I began again, but he hopped off the wall and started walking towards the gate.

'And she doesn't want to know me. It's OK. I've got school tomorrow. D'you need a hand in the morning?'

'No. Summer mornings are easy. But I'd like to take Charlie out again in the evening. Will you ride Woolf?'

'Yup.' He opened the gate and was gone.

I went slowly back indoors. My aunt was driving us both to visit Mum. She didn't mention Kez at all to me, but as soon as we reached the ward where Mum lay, looking brighter but in plaster from thigh to toe, she started. Mum listened to her worried outpourings.

'Fran has done the right thing,' she said firmly. 'We're grateful to you, Eleanor, but you can't help with the animals and Kez sounds invaluable, especially with the horses.'

'But he's a gypsy...' her sister started, and I saw a battling flash of anger in Mum's eyes.

'Then we're doubly lucky to have an expert on our side. Let's hear no more about it, Eleanor. Tell me, how is your husband these days?'

I grinned. Mum, even when confined to a hospital bed, is quite a force to be reckoned with and my aunt indeed said no more about Kez. It was a tricky few days, though, and when at last I knew Mum was coming home I was overjoyed.

Kez was pleased for me, but very quiet. It was a Saturday morning when she came hopping through the kitchen door on crutches. There was a mad, joyful ten minutes of ecstasy from Sam and Shelley and even the snooty cats ran up to her, looking pleased in their inscrutably feline way.

'Come and see the horses.' I virtually dragged her into the yard.

I hoped Kez would be there, doing something wonderful, but instead there was a note pinned to Woolf's door:

'Everything's done. Hope your mum's OK. You won't need me now. There's some comfrey poultice and arnica in the store. See you. Kez.'

SEVEN

MY FACE MUST have fallen. To somewhere around my ankle region I'd say, because Mum said swiftly, 'It's *OK*, Fran.'

I looked at her. 'But we do still need him. How could he go just like that?'

'Either because he feels he's done enough, and Lord knows he's right, *or* because after two weeks of being snubbed and spied on by my dearest sister he's not too keen on meeting me.'

'That's silly,' I said instantly. 'He knows you're brilliant. I told him.'

She balanced precariously on one crutch and hugged me with the other arm. I'd really missed her hugs.

'That's very kind of you, my darling, but Kez might think you're just the teeniest bit prejudiced.'

'You took my word for it about *him* being all right.' I was in a proper huff. 'You were worried to death about "the gypsy boy" looking after the place, but once I said he was OK you believed me.'

'I have complete faith in your judgment,' she said quietly. 'You've had to make a lot of the decisions the way we live and I trust you. If *you* trusted Kez that was good enough for me.'

I hadn't given it any deep thought, but it must have been quite a tough decision for her, lying helpless in hospital as she was.

Although proud that she should have such high regard for me, I still felt hurt and abandoned by Kez. 'So what am I going to do?'

She hobbled energetically to the paddock gate and called the horses. 'Goodness, don't they look well? They're a credit to you, Fran.'

'Thanks, but it wasn't all me, was it?' It was great

having her back, really great, but Kez's vanishing act had cast a gloom over her homecoming. 'Kez has worked really hard on Woolf.'

'I can see he has and I want to thank him. Why don't you go down to the village and see if you can find him? Get him to come and talk to me at least.'

'I can't go chasing after him like that!' I was horrified at the thought.

'Well, I certainly can't.' Mum waved one of the crutches ruefully. 'Go on, Fran, please.'

She kept on and on, and I so wanted Kez back that in the end I agreed. I regretted it, though, as soon as I turned the corner and saw Jake and three of his gang slouched on their garden wall.

They started cat-calling and whistling the minute they spotted me, and when they realised I was heading for the house they really made the most of it.

'Hello, darling! Can't live without him then?' Jake is big and heavy for his age and his flat, pugnacious face was frightening.

I was trembling at the thought of approaching but I held my head high and walked deliberately up the front path.

'Come on, Loverboy. Your snotty girlfriend's here.'

I ignored them all and knocked politely at the door. For a horrible moment I thought Kez wasn't in and I was going to have to turn and walk through the jeering group again. They carried on making crude remarks and I felt my face burning with embarrassment. I was just about to give up when the door was yanked violently open and there was Kez in just a pair of jeans, naked chest gleaming wet and fire leaping from his eyes.

He put a strong hand on my wrist to keep me there and roared, 'That's enough!'

All four of them shut up immediately. Kez brought me

into the house and shut the door on them.

'Sorry, Fran, I was in the shower. What...'

'Mum wants to see you,' I gabbled, too overwhelmingly shy to look at him. 'She's really thrilled at everything you've done and so disappointed you don't want to see us any more. And...and so am I.'

He was still holding me and he squeezed my hand gently. 'I'll get some clothes on.'

I waited in the narrow hall while he ran barefoot upstairs. The house smelled of stale cooking and too many people.

I dreaded having to go past Jake again, but when we walked out of the house, the garden was empty.

I was impressed. 'You got rid of them pretty easily.'

His face hardened. 'And they know enough to keep out of my way for quite a while. They wouldn't have dared say that stuff if they'd known I could hear.'

I thought he was mad at the 'girlfriend' tag and was sad. 'My fault for coming here. Your uncle's not on the phone and I didn't know how else to contact you.'

'I'm glad you did but you shouldn't have to listen to them making comments about you. Put it down to ignorance, they're not used to beautiful girls like you.'

Wow! I felt an immediate glow.

We were walking rapidly towards my house and I told him how delighted Mum was with everything he'd done.

'She's in plaster still, a shorter one now, so she can get about on crutches, but it'll be ages before she can ride.'

He nodded, his face tense and worried.

I put my hand tentatively on his arm. 'Don't worry. She's nothing like Aunt Eleanor.'

He grinned and relaxed a little and I crossed my fingers and toes that he and Mum would click. I needn't have worried. When we arrived she was sitting in a garden chair with the broken leg propped on a bench. Shelley and all *three* cats were in her lap. Sam was lying with his head on her good foot, and there, in our lovely flower garden, the chickens *and* Logic were happily rootling around.

I told her off for that, but she said she'd missed them all so much it was a treat for her as much as for them.

I pretended to grumble. 'I suppose I should be grateful you haven't let the horses tramp across the lawn for a bit of grazing.'

She smiled at that and held her hand out to Kez. 'Talking of gratitude, I owe you a great big bucketful. I honestly don't know how we'd have managed without you. It's thanks to you, not only that I got to the hospital so quickly but that I got any sleep while I was in there. I was sure, you see, that this family of mine were in good hands.'

Nice one, Mum. He looked pleased and embarrassed and relieved all at the same time. I fetched some cold drinks and we sat down and toasted Mum's recovery in home-made lemonade. I watched her and Kez laughing and talking like old friends and nearly burst with happiness. It was wonderful that my mother had trusted my evaluation of Kez, and even better now she'd met him and was agreeing with it one hundred per cent. It wasn't the first time she'd let me make a major decision, but it was probably the bravest from her point of view. I thanked my lucky stars she wasn't ordinary, when being ordinary seemed to mean being narrow and prejudiced, like Aunt Eleanor or even Jake and his mates.

'You're very quiet, Fran.' She pushed her unruly hair from her face and peered at me.

'I'm thinking about being ordinary,' I said, and both she and Kez laughed.

'That's something you're not, for sure.' He pulled a hideous face and I thumped him in a very ungrateful way.

So that was the start of Kez becoming a real part of our small, but select band of friends. He came to the house every day, and although we quickly learned not to keep saying 'thank you' because it embarrassed him, we really didn't know how we'd ever got through before.

It wasn't just looking after the animals and riding Woolf – he could do anything, it seemed. Mum was fascinated by his Romany heritage and encouraged him to talk about his father's family and all they had taught him. She thought they were wonderful people and told him so.

His good-looking face was sad. 'They are, you're right, but unfortunately the fact that dad married a *gorgio* made a difference.'

'What's a *gorgio?*' I thought Kez's mother was from the village.

'A non-Romany. The family liked Mum OK but she wasn't one of them and neither am I. Mum insisted I got a proper schooling, even though we were on the road, so I don't fit in comfortably to their life style. That's why I had to leave when she died.'

I felt a great wave of pity sweep over me but I knew him well enough by now to hide it. 'Will you go back when you're older?'

He shrugged. 'I don't think so. The trouble is I don't fit in anywhere really. Too gypsy for the regular world, too *gorgio* for the Romanies.'

'You could fit in wherever you chose,' Mum said vigorously, hobbling rapidly across the kitchen. She'd progressed to a single stick now, but was still impatient with her improvement. 'You've got to decide what *you* want to do.'

'I want to work with horses, I do know that.' He grinned. 'Even the wicked Woolf hasn't put me off.'

'You should be a vet,' I said. 'Your herbal medicines are terrific. The animals have never been so healthy.'

'I'm not clever enough for the studying.' Kez's blue eyes were serious. 'Anyway I would find it hard to put cats to sleep and destroy unwanted dogs, that kind of thing. It's definitely a job with horses I'd like.'

'A jockey?' Mum sat down with us. 'No, you're too tall. Eventer? Show jumper?'

'I'm not ambitious enough in that line. You've got to be very competitive.'

'Professional trainer. You could break young horses like your dad did,' I said eagerly.

He laughed. 'Thanks for the vote of confidence but it takes years to get that good. I shall probably end up in a factory or something.'

'That would be a wicked waste,' Mum said fiercely. 'How about a blacksmith? Ben's always saying handling the horses is half the skill. The other half can be taught.'

'I'd love that, I've always admired the *kaulomescro*, blacksmith to you, but I can't afford college.'

'I'm sure there's an apprenticeship scheme.' Mum frowned, 'Isn't that what Steve's on, Fran?'

'Mmm.' I still didn't like Steve. 'He works with Ben as a trainee and gets paid, with a one-day release at the local tech.'

'Ideal.' She sounded as if it were all settled. 'I'll talk to Ben about it if you like, Kez. When do you leave school? You're a couple of months older than Fran, I know.'

'Next summer. I've got exams in May, then that's it. I hope I can get something that means I can leave my uncle's. It was good of them to take me in but...' He left it unsaid.

Mum, as usual, was as good as her word and twice as quick. She phoned Ben who'd met Kez by then and they got on well. Most people liked Kez if he gave them the chance and certainly he seemed to have gained a lot of confidence in that line since he'd met us lot. Let's face it if you can take our batty household in your stride, anyone else'd be a doddle.

Ben said he would keep an ear to the ground for any farriers with trainee vacancies. Since hearing about Kez's interest in the trade, Ben called a lot more regularly, always on Steve's college day so that Kez could act as assistant.

'There aren't too many opportunities about, unfortunately,' he told us, as he trimmed Brontë's feet. (She was having the whole summer as a holiday – a complete rest with shoes off.)

'How come?' I asked, 'There seem to be plenty of blacksmiths around.'

'It's a condition of the trainee scheme that you have to be a master farrier and have a permanent smithy somewhere. A lot of the chaps on the circuit just do mobile trade; they don't have a forge as a base. Is that shoe ready, Kez?'

'Think so.' He held out the glowing arc for Ben's inspection.

'Right. That's for Woolf. He's got quite tricky feet, so I'll show you how I shape it.'

I watched Kez's intense face as he followed the farrier's every move. Brontë was waiting to go back into the field and she nudged me impatiently.

'He looks...he looks *happy*, don't you think?' I whispered in her ear but she was never a great one for conversation. Or for cuddles. She put up with the hug I gave her, but no more. Whereas Charlie, my beautiful, gentle Charlie, leaned contentedly against me and sighed with pleasure when I hugged his neck.

Summer was drawing to a close, but there was still time to ride after they'd been shod and we'd had tea. We'd got into the habit, over the months, of inviting Ben to eat and somehow he always managed to make us his last call so that he could stay. He and Mum talked endlessly throughout the meal, and Kez and I would leave them yakking over the washing up while we took the boys out.

'Mum and Ben get on really well,' I remarked as we walked them up the road.

Kez and Woolf had shut the gate, with hardly any trouble, I might add.

'He's a nice bloke. Very sound.' High praise from the straight-as-a-die Kez.

'It would be great if your training course could be with him.' I asked for trot and Charlie struck off perfectly.

Woolf immediately tried to follow, but was firmly checked. 'Not till I ask for it, Fleabrain. I agree, it would be perfect, but there's no chance. Steve only started last winter so he's got another two years at least.'

'Shame. Something will turn up, though, I'm sure.'

He grinned. He did that a lot more frequently nowadays but it still made me feel funny. 'My little Miss Sunshine. Whatever happened to the gloomy girl I met this spring?'

'I wasn't gloomy,' I said indignantly, 'was I?'

'Just a bit.' He laughed at my face. 'Maybe finding out just what a treasure your mum is, made the difference.'

'I've always known that.' I wasn't going to admit it was partly down to having him around that made me feel good. Though we still fall out.'

'I've heard you. Woolf, behave. We'll go round the common and come back along the bridlepath by that wheat field.'

'Where we first got together,' I thought 'how romantic.'

'I want to see how Woolf behaves when you take the lead again,' he continued.

So much for romance. I was glad I hadn't voiced my thoughts aloud.

'Fine with me, but don't you two dare fall down. I couldn't go through that again.'

I cantered Charlie across the common, and to show you how much braver I'd become, I actually got off and

63

towed some logs around to make the jumps *bigger!*

'You're going to have to start competing,' Kez laughed at my exultant expression when we simply flew over.

'Maybe.' I was actually warming to the idea. 'I thought of trying a cross-country in the autumn. Charlie goes so well out in the open. I'd feel more confident than with show jumping.'

'Good idea. Will you stop it, Woolf?' The big bay was pulling like a train to try and get his head in front. 'There's one next month. We'll start training you both for it.'

He made Woolf stay behind us and we had a brilliant race along the sandy track we use for galloping. Woolf's long, racehorsey stride brought him level straightaway, but Charlie gave it his all and we thundered, shoulder to shoulder, all the way. I crouched low over the chestnut horse's neck, the wind in my face, the feel of all that power and speed beneath me. Kez turned his grinning face to mine and we were both laughing exuberantly, drunk with the sheer joy of the moment.

In the end we had to pull them up, as neither would give way and we were running out of track. I eased Charlie down to canter and by the time we reached the wheat field's gate we were smoothly trotting. The grassy track curved away from us, bordering the now bare field. The wheat had been harvested and the soil ploughed in readiness for next year's crop. Far less likelihood of the sudden appearance of a rabbit, but you never know.

Sam and Shelley had caught up with us, after our gallop. They were panting, but they were so fit I knew they were OK to run on. I led the way again, wondering if Charlie would pull or try to bomb off after his exciting race with Woolf, but he obeyed my hands, flexed his neck and cantered smoothly. I could hear the uneven pounding that Woolf's erratic pull-and-tug rocking-horse canter makes, and I glanced over my shoulder. Kez was sitting lightly in the saddle, seeming to hold the big bay effortlessly, but when he caught my look he pulled a hideous face.

'Are you having trouble?' I called. 'Shall I stop?' Mum's accident was horribly fresh in my mind.

'Don't you dare,' he yelled back. 'I *will* get this horse from hell to do as he's told!'

He spoke in a different tone to Woolf, soothing words, which together with the gentle, insistent hands, made the naughty gelding listen. We were nearing the bend where the rabbit had shot out, and I almost held my breath, but then we were rounding it and cantering the straight length that led to the road. Woolf's hoofbeats had settled into a rhythmic canter and when I looked again, he was moving fluidly, curved onto his bridle in a perfect shape, the very picture of a model horse.

I let out my breath and brought Charlie down to walk, and we rode home in the fading light, horses and people in total harmony.

EIGHT

WHEN WE GOT back it was all peace and goodwill at home too. Ben was still there, having helped Mum with the hens and Logic. I thought how kind he was and supposed he felt sorry for her, still hobbling as she was.

He greeted us in his usual cheerful way and said, 'I'm glad you got back before I made a move. Give me a hand with some measurements, would you, Kez? I thought I could make a metal grid for the tack-room window. Come and see what you think.'

Mum limped over to take Woolf. She was really missing the riding, I knew, and liked at least to give her bad boy his food and lots of cuddling.

'I don't want him forgetting me.' She gave him a swift once over and asked as usual how the ride had gone.

I decided against mentioning the 'accident track' but told her all about the jumps and the gallop. She looked wistful and shifted her injured leg impatiently.

To change the subject I said quickly, 'Why is Ben making an iron grille for the tack-room?'

'Apparently there are some thieves operating in the area. Ben says our door is solid enough, though he's going to put another lock on it, but he knows they've got into a couple of places by simply breaking the window.'

I was alarmed. 'We'd better keep the saddles in the kitchen till he's fixed it then.'

'D'you think that's necessary?' She frowned and ran her fingers through her fringe as usual.

'Yes, I do,' I said, as patiently as I could. 'And leave your hair alone. It looks nice today.'

'Don't boss me around...'

'*Here we go, here we go, here we go-o,*' Kez sang, grinning broadly at us. 'What are you fighting about now?'

'Fran thinks we should keep the tack indoors till you've burglar-proofed the store.'

'And she's right.' Ben patted my head approvingly. 'Some of my customers have lost the lot in the past few weeks.'

'Horrible thought, thieves sneaking round the place.' I shuddered. 'They wouldn't dare try the house with the noise Sam makes. But what about the horses, Ben? We've had them both freeze-marked and got padlocks on all the gates.'

'I haven't heard of anyone losing any animals. This lot seem to specialise in tack theft – they're in, out and gone. I'm glad you've got the horses marked though. If Charlie's last owner had done that he wouldn't have lost him, would he?'

There was a stunned silence. At least from Mum and me.

Kez looked uncomfortable. 'I don't think it's occurred to Fran and her mum that Charlie's probably stolen.'

'I paid for him!' Mum threw her hands up and Woolf shied with his back end, keeping his head firmly in the feed bucket. 'Sorry, Woolfie.' She patted him and looked at me appealingly. 'Fran knows I did.'

'Of course. Mum handed over a month's housekeeping in cash.'

'And I've got a receipt,' she remembered triumphantly.

I thought of the grubby scrap of paper with a scrawled signature on it. 'Yes. Yes, she has.'

'I didn't mean *you* stole him, Jane,' Ben smiled at her outraged face and pretended to punch her chin. 'The nasty bit of work you bought him from. Didn't you think it was odd that a man like that would own, legitimately own, a horse like Charlie?'

I drew a breath. Now he'd said it, it was obvious. I'd been so busy nursing the chestnut back to health then enjoying the sheer pleasure of owning and riding him, I had pushed any such thought away. Mum hadn't done any pushing. The idea that she'd bought a stolen horse had never, ever dawned on her.

I flopped down suddenly on the yard bench. 'He's not mine! Charlie's not mine!'

'Don't be so dramatic, Fran.' she sounded quite cross. 'We've just established that I paid for him.'

'But that man didn't own him. Charlie wasn't his to sell.' I was on the verge of tears and I hadn't cried for ages.

'I can't believe that.' She looked imploringly at Ben. 'You don't really believe it, do you?'

'Jane, you are too pure for the real world.' Ben was being very gentle with her. 'Yes, I'm afraid I do believe it. The horse is well bred, good-looking and beautifully schooled. Extremely valuable I'd say, wouldn't you, Kez?'

Kez nodded his dark head slowly. 'Worth a lot more than the housekeeping money, that's for sure.'

'But I thought...' Mum ran her hands frenziedly through her hair, making its for once smooth waves stand out in a wild mane. 'I thought the dreadful man was one of those travellers everyone hates. Real gypsies look after their horses so I knew he wasn't Romany, just a cruel and ignorant copy.'

I couldn't stop crying. I was saying over and over, 'We should have known.'

Ben and Kez looked at each other with despair.

'Well, you didn't know.' The blacksmith tried to jolly us along. 'You bought him in good faith, so he's yours, isn't he?'

'But someone out there *really* owns him.' I tried to wipe away the tears. 'I can't keep Charlie knowing there's probably a girl breaking her heart at losing him.'

'Come on, Fran. We could be wrong.' Kez sat beside me and put a comforting arm round me. 'And it's too late now. The bloke who sold him to your mum is long gone. Without him we can't find out where Charlie came from.'

'We'll have to put an advert in the paper.' Mum had gone as pale as I felt. 'With a picture of the horse and a description.'

'He can't be from round here,' Ben said and I saw he'd put *his* arm round her. 'The local press won't be any good. Kez is right, what's done is done. Just be glad you were the ones to buy Charlie.'

I sniffed and took Kez's hanky gratefully. 'His real owner will have called him something else.' For some reason the thought started me off again.

'Don't cry any more, Fran.' Mum begged, and I could see her lip begin to tremble too. 'We'll put an ad in the national horsey magazines and we'll tell the police too.'

Ben scratched his head. 'I don't get it. It will break both your hearts if you have to give up the horse. Why don't you leave it?'

'Because we can imagine what it must be like to have a horse stolen.' Mum said. 'And that must be more than heart-breaking.'

'I wish I'd never mentioned it.' Poor Ben looked at Kez, who nodded in sympathy.

I had rested my head on his shoulder, my face hidden against his neck. I was grateful he'd never voiced the possibility of my beautiful chestnut horse being stolen. At least I'd had six wonderful months of happiness.

I went drearily through the evening's routine and as soon as Kez left, I took to my bed. Ben had stayed, he was truly concerned at how upset we both were and I could hear the murmur of his deep, comfortable voice in the kitchen as I cried myself to sleep.

The next morning Mum had a hospital appointment to check the broken leg. I wished her luck and went off, still red-eyed and unhappy, to school.

Kelly spotted my sad face and rushed over at break to see what was up. 'That Kez hasn't thrown you over has he, honey?'

I managed a small smile at that. 'I've told you, he's not my boyfriend. No, it's Charlie.'

I told her all about the revelation that he was probably stolen.

She was unimpressed. 'What's there to cry about? You bought him, you own him, end of story. Whoever this guy pinched him from hasn't come looking, has he?'

I shook my head.

'They probably claimed the insurance money and bought another horse the next day.' Kelly's very practical. 'It's only zappy types like you and your ma who get all sentimental.'

'You're horrible.' She made me laugh, though. 'And I don't know what's worse, being called zappy or senti-mental!'

'Ask your pig. He'll tell you it's worse being called Logic.' She fell about at that, but I was thinking about Charlie's owner again. I kept picturing a girl like me, going out to her field one day and finding it empty. Her beautiful, dearly loved chestnut horse stolen, beaten and bullied into a lorry and carted off somewhere to be teth-ered and starved.

Tears came flooding back and Kelly looked at me with horror.

'What the heck did I say?'

'I wondered what Charlie's real owner called him,' I explained, hiccuping as I tried to stop crying.

'Take my advice and don't give it another thought.' Kelly patted my back kindly. 'Quick, dry up before the rest of the class see you. They think you're tapped already.'

'You're a real pal, aren't you!' I stuck my tongue out at her, but mopped up and got through the rest of the day without bawling.

Kelly's a boarder but she always walks to the gate with

me when school's finished so we can have a last-minute gossip.

That day she looked across the road and said, 'Wowee! He can do my homework any time he likes!'

I followed her gaze and blushed violently. 'That's Kez.'

'Phew.' She gave his tall, lean figure the once-over. 'Tell him if he's ever in California to look me up. You lucky devil, Fran.'

'I told you...' I fiddled with my hair. 'He's *not* my boyfriend.'

'Yeah, yeah. You look fine by the way. And I bet you're real cute together.'

I hissed at her to shut up and walked nonchalantly over to join Kez.

'Bye, Frannie!' Kelly waved and jumped up and down.

'Who's your shy little friend?' Kez gave her a brief, but devastating smile, and took my bag off my shoulder. 'What have you got in here, lead weights?'

'Geography and English Lit. And her name's Kelly.' I passed on the message about California and he shuddered.

'Don't think so, somehow.'

I was pleased. I liked Kelly a lot, but I didn't particularly want him to.

'So, to what do I owe this honour?' I thought he was trying to cheer me up about Charlie and was determined to do my best in that line. 'You've never met me from school before.'

'No.' He was hesitant. 'I called at the house first and I...just thought it would be better if I spoke to you before you got home.'

I might be slow about some things but I knew this was trouble. 'What is it?' I asked swiftly. 'Charlie? Has his owner turned up?'

'No. *No*, I said. Fran, calm down. I don't want you to be upset, but it's your mum.'

71

'Another accident? She's had another...'

'I'll tell you if you let me.' He was very patient. 'She went to hospital today for another check and they're not happy with the leg. She's going to need another operation.'

I closed my eyes. 'Oh, poor Mum. She hates being in hospital.'

'But she hates not being able to walk more. Without this operation her leg will never be OK.'

'So no more riding ever.' I knew how much she missed it. 'Then it's worth going through, isn't it? Why did you think I'd be so upset?'

'They want her in very soon and guess who's the only person available to house-sit?'

I stared at him. 'Oh no, not...'

'Yup. Good old Aunty Eleanor.'

'What about Dad?' I demanded. 'I told him what my aunt was like and he said he'd stay with me if anything else happened.'

'He's in America again,' Kez said. 'Your mum tried him first.'

'I've hardly seen him this summer.' I was feeling sorry for myself. 'He's thinking of settling in Arizona, you know.'

'Nice. Think of the great holidays you'll be able to have.'

'True. But it doesn't help us now, does it? How long will the operation take?'

'I think she'll be in hospital a week,' Kez said. 'But don't go all gloomy on her, will you? She's more upset at leaving you with her fearsome sister than she is about her leg.'

I felt ashamed. I shouldn't have to be told to put my own mother before my selfish little self, should I?

'You're much nicer than me, aren't you?' I said to Kez, and he roared with laughter.

'Tell that to Jake. I caught him pinching some of my decoctions and I clouted him so hard he's got a cauliflower ear this morning.'

'What was he taking?' I was intrigued.

'Stuff made from burdock root. It's good for skin problems. I'd have let him have it if he'd asked, but as he didn't I gave his skin something else to worry about.'

He looked grimly satisfied and I was glad he was on my side, not against me. We reached home and I think I did the concerned daughter bit very well.

'And you're sure you don't mind Eleanor coming?' Mum had hugged me several times and was watching me anxiously.

I crossed my fingers and said cheerfully, 'Not a bit. She's very kind to do it. As long as she doesn't try to make me eat pork chops again we'll get on fine.'

'I've told her Kez is to come in whenever he wants,' she went on. 'And I've made loads of your favourite lasagnes. They're in the freezer.'

'You're a darling,' I told her. 'Just get in that hospital and come home with two working legs.'

Ben took her in a few days later, and when I got home from school, there was my aunt. She'd re-arranged the furniture and dusted *inside* the cupboards, but I realised this time how much she missed her own immaculate flat and didn't sigh about it. We'd persuaded Kez to meet her, but after two days of chilly politeness on my aunt's part and tongue-tied silence on his, he gave up and stayed outside when he called.

The evenings had drawn in and most of our riding out was done at weekends now, but we schooled the horses regularly and Charlie and I practised our jumping when we could. I'd decided not to think about his ownership for the time being; I had enough to worry me anywayt, what with Mum's operation and the cross-country coming up.

I was concerned one night when the stitching on Charlie's throatlash buckle unravelled and it was

73

impossible to fasten it properly. I showed it to Kez.

'I can fix it,' he said instantly. 'I've got some tools at home. I'll bring them up tomorrow.'

'Thank you,' I said, but he was very quick to detect something was wrong.

'That's too late, I suppose? You really want to do those solid jumps after school, don't you? OK, I'll take the bridle home and do it tonight.'

'You *are* lovely.' I beamed at him and he flicked water from the trough all over me. I'd forgotten the golden rule – don't praise Kez. I knew I was right, though, he *was* lovely.

I watched him set off with the bridle over his shoulder, then gritted my teeth and settled down to watch TV with my aunt. She knitted all though the programmes and the clicking sound drove me mad. I was highly relieved when the phone rang and she put the wool down.

'Yes,' I heard her say, 'this is the Harper household. Well, we *know* him, of course. He says what? No, that can't be right. Hold the line please.' She put her hand over the mouthpiece and hissed at me. 'Fran. It's your so-called friend.'

'So-called...' I stared at her.

'The gypsy. Kez or whatever you call him.'

'Let me talk to him.' I held out my hand, annoyed.

She pulled away. 'It's not him. It's the police. He's at the station. They've arrested him.'

NINE

To say I was stunned is an understatement. I gawped at her: 'What...what do they say he's done?'

'He was found with some property on him which he says is ours.'

'Property?' Realisation dawned and I said thankfully 'It's Charlie's bridle. Kez took it home to mend it. Tell them I asked him to.'

She spoke briefly into the phone, then said, 'Certainly not. I'm not prepared to turn out now.'

I looked at her with dawning horror as she put the receiver firmly back. 'What did they want you to do?'

'Go down to the police station and identify the bridle. Quite ridiculous at this time of night.'

I looked at the clock. It wasn't even nine.

'But we've got to,' I stammered. 'If we don't go there and prove Kez is telling the truth they'll think he's a thief.'

She shrugged. She didn't say it then, but her look said 'He probably is'.

I wanted to scream. Instead I picked up the phone and dialled Ben's number. It rang for ages and I felt my heart sink further and further, then at last he answered.

I gulped and gabbled the story and to his great credit he grasped the seriousness of it all.

'I'll come and get you now,' he said immediately. 'And we'll go to the station together.'

I was so angry I couldn't speak to my aunt. I simply left the room and went out to the porch to wait for Ben. He lives in the next village, about four miles away, so he wasn't long. I ran out and jumped in the car.

'Does your aunt know where we're going?'

I shook my head and he nipped swiftly indoors to speak to her.

He drove off and patted my shoulder reassuringly. 'Don't look so tragic. It's just a misunderstanding, that's all. We'll soon sort it.'

'It shouldn't happen,' I burst out. 'They wouldn't assume Kez was a thief if he wasn't a gypsy.'

'Not at all. The police would investigate any young fellow found with someone else's stuff on him.'

'But my aunt should have spoken up for him.' I was clenching and unclenching my fists.

'She doesn't know him. She didn't *want* to know him which we find odd, but let's face it, when it came to warm and lovable your mum got her sister's share.'

I smiled at that.

He went on, 'Much better that I go along and speak up. I can totally vouch for Kez's honesty. He wouldn't take as much as a nail of mine. Unlike that little toe-rag Steve. I'm always losing bits and pieces when he's around, but Kez is absolutely straight.'

'Thank you, Ben.' I blinked away the tears of rage. 'And I can vouch that he has Charlie's bridle with my permission so it'll be all right, won't it?'

It was, of course. I will admit my heart nearly stopped when we walked in and I saw the blank eyes in Kez's white face. Hope sprang in them as soon as he saw us, and by the time the police had sorted out who we were and what we were doing, they were almost back to their usual blue brilliance. The experience marked him though. He was bitter that it would colour public opinion of him, even though he had proved to be innocent. I thought he'd be particularly angry with Aunt Eleanor, but he took the same attitude as Ben.

'She doesn't know me.' He even managed a smile at my outraged face. 'Or my people. She thinks all gypsies are thieves.'

I was never going to forgive my aunt.

76

After Ben had brought me back from the police station I'd stomped into the living room, picked up Pinter, and marched straight upstairs. Aunt Eleanor had followed me up to my bedroom.

'It's no good getting in a temper with me, Francesca. I've made no secret of the fact that I disapprove of this...liaison you and your mother have with the gypsy. And now I'm proved right.'

I stared in amazement at her smug face. 'What are you talking about? I told you Kez had that bridle because I asked him to mend it.'

'But the police wouldn't have arrested him if they weren't already suspicious of him. Let's face it, he's the obvious suspect for these tack thefts. You said yourself he knows all about saddlery.'

'He knows all about loads of things.' I honestly could have slapped her. 'And the police *didn't* arrest him. A local patrol car saw him turning into the estate with the bridle and knew no one living there was likely to own a horse. They would have stopped anyone in the circumstances. All they said was "Is that your property?" and of course he said no, so they had to check it out.'

She sniffed. 'I still say there's more to it than that. He is a gypsy after all. I expect he knows where all the horses are round here, and probably where their tack is kept too. Look how he used to hang round this house! And you've just said he can even fix saddlery up, so he could sell anything he stole.'

'How dare you!' I was too upset to argue coherently. 'You're making up a case against Kez because you're narrow and bigoted.'

'Better than being gullible and stupid,' she snapped back. 'You and Jane are already in trouble, buying that stolen horse. You'd think you two would have learned your lesson, but no, you have to go and bail out that thieving gypsy.'

That was another night when I cried myself to sleep. Her cruel comments about Kez and my darling Charlie had cut deep and I couldn't keep them to myself. Mum was distressed too, when I told her the whole story the next day in hospital.

'She always did have a wicked tongue when she lost her temper. I'm so sorry, darling, you'll just have to keep out of her way for one more day, then I'll be home. I'll try and make her apologise to you *and* Kez, but I don't hold out much hope. She does have a kind heart but she doesn't know how to use it.'

I did as she said and tried to dismiss my aunt's vitriol from my mind, but it was hard. I realised that a lot of people might think, like her, that there was no smoke without fire, and that Kez *was* involved in the spate of tack theft. He's very bright of course, and although I didn't ever tell him what my aunt had said, he knew the suspicions that she and other people had.

'I would love to be able to find this gang,' he said grimly the next day. 'It's someone with a lot of local knowledge, you know. One poor family has been done *twice*. They replaced all the stolen stuff with brand new and now they've lost that too.'

Ben had just arrived. He was going to bring Mum back from the hospital and had called for her clothes.

'That's right,' he said, shaking his head. 'They're customers of mine, you know. They'd moved the stuff to a store nearer the house, but hadn't even got round to insuring it – couldn't believe that lightning would strike twice.'

'Poor things,' I said with feeling. 'I hope I've remembered everything, Ben. It's all in this case.'

'I'm sure you have. Are you coming with me?'

'No, we're the 'welcome home' party,' I said. 'I can't wait

to see her here.'

Aunt Eleanor had, of course, left the place thoroughly scrubbed and spring-cleaned before she'd driven huffily off. So there was no housework, but plenty to do. Kez and I had made a big banner and we fixed it over the door with dozens of brightly coloured balloons, and we strung Christmas lights in the magnolia tree by the gate. Then we made a great plate of snacks and put some ice in a bucket for the *pièce de résistance* – a bottle of champagne. Well, not exactly champagne but it had gold foil round the top and lots of bubbles.

I put big bows round the necks of Sam, Shelley, Pinter, Willow and Ayckbourn. The cats kept pulling at theirs, but when Kez tried one on Logic he loved it and trotted about looking important if slightly bizarre. There wasn't much we could do with the chickens, but we got some corn to scatter as we ran to the car, so they'd follow us and it would look as if they were joining in the welcome greeting. I found some tinsel for the horses' manes and tails, and we'd just finished when we heard Ben's car arrive.

Mum's face when she saw the big 'WELCOME HOME WE ALL MISSED YOU' banner and us, the dogs, cats, chickens and pig all rushing towards her, was an absolute picture. She drank the 'champagne' and shared her sandwiches with Woolf, Brontë and Charlie who were in the yard waiting for her.

'It's a wonderful homecoming.' There were happy tears in her eyes. 'Thank you all so much.'

'But you're still on crutches.' I was very disappointed. Although I'd seen her limping around in hospital, I'd somehow thought she'd coming running up our path to join us.

'Only for a little while.' She gave me a loving smile and yet another hug. 'The doctors are very pleased with me. I

79

have to go to physio for a while to get the muscles working and once I have their approval...guess what?'

'You can ride?' I was thrilled for her.

'Yes. Very gently, mind. I told them about Brontë and they said she sounds ideal. They weren't too keen on the sound of Woolf.'

Kez put his hands over the big bay's ears. 'Don't listen, mate. I can't think why they don't want you as a therapy horse!'

We all laughed and my eyes met Kez's. We were both delighted for Mum, she'd missed riding so much, but we'd both secretly dreaded being told Kez wasn't needed to ride Woolf any more.

As if she could read our minds (and I sometimes think she can) Mum said, 'From what I hear the wicked Woolf's improved beyond belief anyway. That's why I don't want you to stop riding him, Kez. Even when I'm fit enough I'd still like you to take him out, if you would. You're good for him.'

Kez looked embarrassed as usual, but very, very pleased. He carried on coming to see us every day, and he was also there to cheer Charlie and me on when the day came for our first cross-country. We'd decided to take Woolf along too. Kez thought the experience would be good for him, and of course he'd be invaluable as travelling companion to Charlie. Weeks of patience had paid off and the chestnut would now walk willingly into the trailer, but he was much happier if his friend Woolf was there with him.

The course wasn't too big, though solidly built. I hoped Charlie wouldn't be put off by my knees which were wobbling like jelly. Once we got going, though, I was OK and we sailed over the steeply undulating fields, taking everything literally in our stride. Kez followed a few horses later, but came to grief at the rails where Woolf refused to do a 'double bounce' in and out.

'Perfectly simple jump,' Kez grumbled, brushing the mud off his sleeve. 'He's done the same kind of thing a hundred times, but today he decided he couldn't do it on a hill and stopped dead.'

'You don't usually fall off when he does that.' I tried not to sound superior (Charlie and I had simply flown that one!)

'I didn't fall off today.' He glared at me. 'At least not until Peabrain here decided to cat-jump it from a standstill. *Then* I fell off'.

'Poor Kez. I think you were truly brave to enter at all on Woolf.' Mum, only limping slightly now, was being our 'groom'. 'How d'you think Fran and Charlie are doing?'

'There are quite a few clears but nothing to touch Fran for time. Old Charlie boy can certainly motor.'

'It's all that racing-on-the-common practice,' I was feeling excited. I hadn't thought beyond getting round the course but now it looked as if we might actually get a place!

Imagine how I felt when the recorded times were announced and '...in first place Charlie, owned and ridden by Miss Francesca Harper.' I think I screamed. I know Mum did.

We talked and talked about it all the way home and when I drifted off to sleep that night, still clutching our cup, I decided I was going to be an eventer. Me!

'Better keep practising.' Kez winked at Mum when I told him. 'You and Charlie are going to have to jump a lot higher than that.'

He didn't mean to but he brought me swiftly down to earth. I couldn't do it without Charlie; he was the first horse I'd ever had confidence in, but was he actually owned by me? It was a major worry and one we just had to resolve.

We'd put together an ad for the national horsey mags. It read 'DO YOU KNOW THIS HORSE?' above a nice photo of Charlie taken in the summer. Below it we'd put a brief but accurate description of his markings and our phone number.

'I know we've got to do it,' I told Kez, 'but I shall die every time the phone rings.'

For a few weeks I did just that (well, OK, not literally) but gradually the horror of it faded. As Kez said, we'd done our best and if no one got in touch either via the ad or the police, then we'd just have to assume Charlie was ours.

My dad came back from America for a while and I went over to spend a few days at his house. I came back, thrilled to bits with the present he'd brought me from Arizona.

I rushed into the yard to tell Mum. She was holding Woolf while Ben and Steve worked on his off-fore shoe. 'Is he all right?' They'd only been shod the week before.

'Fine.' Mum hugged me one-handed. 'The dope's trodden on his own shoe and pulled it off, I think. Did you have a good time? We missed you.'

I could feel Steve sneering so I disentangled myself and said, 'Yes. Dad took me to the theatre in London and that sort of stuff. And look what he brought back from the US.'

I fetched the incredibly beautiful Western-style saddle he'd presented me with.

'Phew,' Ben whistled appreciatively. 'That's worth a few bob.'

'I shan't sell it. It's the right size for Charlie, Dad took his measurements over. I shall learn to ride Western style.'

'I'll get you some chaps,' Mum said, smoothing the intricately carved leather. 'I knew he was getting it, but I didn't realise it would be so wonderful, Fran.'

'You two go and catch up on all your news.' Ben

82

grinned at us. 'We'll put Woolf back in his field.'

I put the gorgeous saddle away and Mum and I walked back to the house. She was moving really well now and had some lovely funny stories about her rides on Brontë to entertain me with. Ben stuck his head in the kitchen door.

'We're off. Woolf's back to rights. Oh, by the way, your window grille's breaking apart in one corner. I've put it in the van so I can mend it at the forge. I'll bring it back tomorrow.'

'Thanks, Ben.' We started getting the tea and I listened for Kez's arrival. My heart did its usual gymnastics when his dark face appeared and I realised how much I'd missed him. He didn't hug me like Mum had, but he pulled my hair in an affectionate way, I thought. It took a while to get the chickens away that night because Stella and Katy had gone walkabout and it was starting to get dark as we walked towards the yard to bring the horses in for the night. I was highly surprised when there was a scrunch of gravel behind us and Ben's van pulled up.

'Hiya,' I said. 'Forgot something?'

He got out, looking quite serious. 'Come back to the house just for a minute,' he said. 'I'd like to talk to you all.'

I felt worried. It wasn't like our good-tempered Ben to look so stern.

'These tack thefts,' he began, and I saw Kez's fists clench. He'd never got over the night the police had thought he might be the culprit.

Mum saw his face and leaned forward. 'Don't look like that, Kez. I've said sorry in a thousand different ways that my sister was such a...a rat. I was very hard on her; she's still reeling.'

'So she should be,' I said passionately. 'It was her fault Kez was arrested and...'

'I wasn't arrested and it wasn't her fault. Don't be so dramatic Miss Academy Award.' Kez batted me lightly.

'She should have...' I began again but Ben interrupted.

'It's not about that anyway. It's just – I've had an idea, but it's completely up to you whether we carry it through.'

'Fire away,' Mum said.

'It was seeing Fran's new saddle. It really is quite valuable and I thought it would be the perfect bait.'

'Bait?' I wasn't keen on the word.

'If we let it be known there's several hundred pounds worth of tack sitting in a store room with an unguarded window we just might draw the thieves out. It's obvious they're local and equally obvious they're being tipped off by someone.'

'Unguarded!' I squeaked suddenly. 'The grille's off the tack-room window! My saddle's out there!'

I jumped up but Ben put out a restraining hand. 'I took it off deliberately. Kez is going to drop the hint casually, as it were, amongst the village lads. If I'm right, someone will pass the news on and the thieves won't be able to resist it.'

I stared at him in disbelief. 'You're going to encourage them to pinch my saddle? My gorgeous new saddle?!'

TEN

'IT'S A GREAT idea!' Kez is so much quicker than me. 'I let it be known that Fran's got a brand new, very pricey saddle – and that the window grille's away till morning. They won't be able to resist easy pickings like that and they're bound to make a grab for it tonight.'

'But...' I squealed again and he put a finger to my lips. 'But we'll be there – Ben and I – hidden in the tack-room, just waiting for them.'

Mum and I stared at the two of them. 'You don't mean it?'

'I certainly do,' Ben said grimly. 'Kez has got it dead right.'

'But it sounds so dangerous.' Mum looked truly concerned and I thought how nice that she was so fond of them both.

'We can look after ourselves, don't worry.' Ben flexed a muscular arm and grinned at her. 'And we'll have the advantage of a surprise attack.'

'Attack!' She was even more perturbed. 'What d'you think's going to happen? I can't understand why you want to take such a risk, Ben. These thefts aren't your problem.'

'Maybe not directly, but apart from the fact I hate to sit by and watch the distress these swine are causing, there's Kez.'

Kez nodded in agreement, his eyes hard. 'The only way I can hope to clear my name completely is to nail the real thieves.'

'Do people still think you're involved?' Mum demanded, and he nodded again.

'Oh yes. Like your sister, they're very ready to believe the worst. They know the police let me go, but the stealing still goes on and some still think it's me.'

'It's so unfair...' I started, but he took me by the shoulders and shook me gently.

'Life *is* unfair, Francesca. I know I'll always have to work that bit harder to be accepted by some people. I don't mind that, but I do mind being labelled a thief. I'm really lucky to have you three rooting for me.'

I beamed at him. 'And together we can help clear your name. Put like that it's worth it, isn't it, Mum?'

She still didn't seem totally convinced, I think the expression "surprise attack" was worrying her. The expression "steal Fran's saddle" wasn't doing a lot for me either, but I pushed the thought away as ignoble.

We worked on Mum a bit longer until she finally agreed to the plan. Then we brought in the horses and she and I fed them while Ben drove the van round the back of the house to hide it. Kez nipped off home to spread the word about my fabulous new saddle.

He was back a couple of hours later, appearing silently in the blue-black of the winter's evening. He slipped indoors and into the bright warmth of our big kitchen.

'You look cold.' Mum fussed round him. 'Come over to the stove and have a hot drink.'

He took the mug and drank, raising his eyebrows wickedly at me over its rim.

'Mum wanted you and Ben to wear big quilted sleeping bags,' I said, all straight-faced. 'But Ben drew a very pretty picture of you both trying to run after the burglars with your feet all wrapped inside.'

He spluttered into the drinking chocolate. 'Like detectives in a sack race!'

'I was only thinking of you,' Mum tried to be dignified. 'You don't know how long you're going to be waiting in that store, and it's freezing out there.'

'I've got a hot-waterbottle they can have,' I offered. 'And

a teddy bear.'

Mum and Kez bashed me simultaneously.

'Don't take the mickey, you,' Ben said, grinning. 'Just because you'll be tucked up in your nice warm bed.'

'Oh no, I won't,' I said. 'I'm coming with you.'

'No chance,' Kez said immediately, and Mum shook her head emphatically.

'That's nice of you, Fran,' Ben's always so kind. 'But it could get a bit rough. Far too dangerous to risk involving you.'

'But I am involved,' I argued. 'It's my saddle!'

'Fran, that's enough!' Mum sounded quite sharp. She'd become much more grown up and responsible since her accident I'd noticed. 'You are *not* spending the night hiding in the tack-room.'

'Not the tack-room,' I said impatiently. 'The stable. Using a saddle as bait is one thing but if we've enticed a bunch of thieves to call there's no way I'm risking losing the horses.'

'This lot don't steal horses...' Ben began, but I was in full flight.

'They might want to when they see ours. And even if they don't I'll be near enough to see what happens to you and Kez in the store. You can't hear anything that goes on in our yard from the house. I can signal to Mum and she can phone the police.'

'If you think I'm letting you prance around shining torches or blowing whistles when there's a surprise attack going on, you've got another thought coming.' Mum glared at me and I glared back.

'And if you think I'm going to stay meekly indoors while someone steals Woolf, Brontë and Charlie *you've* got another...'

'Whoa, whoa. Calm down you two.' Ben spoke as if he was gentling naughty and excitable horses. 'Let's discuss

87

this properly.'

'There's nothing to discuss.' Mum ruffled her hair savagely and he stroked it back in place.

'Don't do that. Listen, Jane, Fran's got a point. If we have any trouble we might need the police in a hurry.'

'I'm not having her running about in that yard!'

'No, I agree. But if she's hidden safely in one of the stables, there's my mobile phone. Fran can take that in with her and as soon as she hears anything she can dial nine, nine, nine.'

'They'll hear her,' Mum objected.

'Not if she's in the far end one, Charlie's stable,' Kez said. 'You know you're not going to keep her in here while she thinks something might happen to the horses.'

He smiled at me and I felt the usual warm glow.

Ben said, 'He's right, Jane. We all know what a determined little character she is. And it will be a help to have back-up if these blighters put up any resistance.'

'You're sure Fran won't be in danger?' Mum looked anxiously at me. 'I could wait with her but you said you'd need someone in the house.'

'I do. A further insurance in case they get away from us. Fran can phone you and you can watch from the top window and see what car they take off in.'

'Quite a military operation,' I said with satisfaction and Ben narrowed his eyes at me.

'And I'm the commander, remember. You obey my orders absolutely and you'll be in no danger whatsoever.'

'Yes, sir,' I said, quite happy to be obedient now I'd got my way.

'Right.' Kez put down his mug and pulled the labrador's ears. 'You're back-up defence too, Sam, my friend. We'd take you with us but I think you'd give the game away.'

'OK, troops? Shall we get ready?' Ben picked up

blankets and a heavy flashlight. 'Better make a flask for yourself Fran. Strong coffee to keep you awake. It could be a long night.'

Keep me awake! He must be joking. I felt sick and shaky and excited all at once. We went out to the yard. The air felt cold and clouds moved heavily across the moon's face. My torch carved a thin channel through the dense blackness as we walked quietly towards the store. Ben didn't want to use his heavy lamp.

'Just in case anyone's snooping around,' he whispered.

We unlocked the heavy tack-room door, and he and Kez settled down in the farthest corner. A break in the clouds sent a sudden shower of moonlight, bathing the quiet yard in its eerie glow. I waited for darkness again and shone my torch, burglar-like, through the window. I swept the beam around the store and, after adjusting the hanging New Zealand rugs so they completely obscured the far corner, was satisfied that the thieves wouldn't see anything to make them suspicious. What they undoubtedly would see was my new saddle. Even by torchlight you could pick out its rich glow and I did my finger and toe crossing act that it would still be there in the morning.

I pushed open the tack-room door a little and hissed 'It's perfect. Can't see you at all. I'm closing the door now.'

'Go straight to Charlie's stable and stay there, mind.' Ben's disembodied voice floated through the dark. 'And don't come out till I tell you.'

'Yes, sir,' I said again, and heard Kez's quiet chuckle.

I pulled the door shut – it had a double Yale lock on it now – and pattered swiftly across the block to the end stable. Brontë was pulling contentedly at her hay with Willow curled warmly beside her as usual. The mare merely rolled an eye to see who was going by but Woolf and Charlie both hung their heads over the door and blew warm whickers of greeting. I stroked the bay's nose and gave him a handful of pony nuts.

'Go back in and keep out of trouble,' I told him and slipped the bolt on Charlie's door.

I'd slept in a stable before, ages ago when I sat up all night with a mildly colicky Brontë, and had rather liked it. The clean smell of hay and straw mingle, and the horse emanates such warmth it feels quite cosy, even on the coldest night. That night was certainly cold and I did have a sleeping bag to help the cosy bit along. Charlie was very pleased to see me, especially with the unusual treat of pony nut titbits, and he spent some time nudging me curiously and nuzzling my hair.

It was very, very dark. Your eyes acclimatise after a while, but a winter night in the country is still incredibly black. In town there are always street lights, or even if none nearby, the glow from the thousands of houses always lightens the deepest of February skies. If, like us, there's just a little village down the road, a moonless sky stays determinedly unlit. I sat in my quilt amongst the straw, just able to make out the shape of Charlie's bulk as he moved peacefully around the box. The slightly sick feeling of excitement had abated and I was glad Ben had suggested bringing the flask. I would never have believed I'd feel sleepy sitting upright in a stable waiting for a visit from a villainous band of thieves, but as the time wore on, I did. I drank some of the coffee, telling myself it would keep me awake. Then I told myself the concentration of listening for the thieves' arrival would keep me awake. Then I told myself – I can't remember what but it certainly didn't work because I fell asleep.

I woke with a terrifying start. A strange rasping noise had roused me and I crept carefully out of the sleeping bag to investigate. Charlie was still pulling quietly at his hay.

I moved close to him and he stopped munching to nudge me in his usual friendly way. The clouds had thinned while I slept, and they now drifted raggedly across the moon's face, filtering patches of light across the yard. I edged carefully to the door and, flattening myself against the wall, peered cautiously over. I could see the gate quite clearly now, still securely shut and padlocked. Brontë's grey head appeared briefly over her door, and the odd, rhythmic noise still went on. I was about to panic and ring someone on the mobile, when a thought struck me.

I moved away from the door and crossed quietly to the stable's inner wall. It's the one adjoining Woolf's box and as soon as I put my ear to the wall and the sound became louder and clearer, I knew what it was. Woolfie was snoring. He's a very relaxed sleeper, flat out on his side with nose buried in the straw. I could picture the contented expression on his handsome, snoring face. I curbed a mad desire to giggle and crept back to the door.

It was cold outside my sleeping bag but I wanted the sharp air to keep me conscious. I thought five minutes or so of standing there would make falling asleep again totally impossible. I was just about to turn back to my warm corner when a feint sound from further down the yard made me freeze, though not with cold.

The moon had sailed behind her veil of clouds again and I couldn't see as far as the end stable and the tack-room. A feint grey shape appeared, Brontë being nosy again, but I was sure I could hear movement from beyond her. I squinted through the enveloping blackness, then stiffened suddenly. A bright pinpoint of light had appeared, bringing the tack-room window clearly into view. Someone was out there. Someone who was shining a torch through the unprotected window, just the way I had a few hours earlier.

I held my breath, terror gripping me for an instant. I felt as though whoever it was peering through the glass to look at my wonderful new saddle, could see me too. Ridiculous, of course, and luckily I realised it and calmed down before I screamed and threw my flask at him or something. I stayed where I was, pressed back against the wall, and strained my ears and eyes as hard as I could. The light wavered a little as it moved slowly, shining on every corner and angle of the store.

I prayed silently that Ben and Kez were still completely hidden behind the rugs, and when the torch clicked out and reappeared at the yard gate, I knew the thief was satisfied. It was still pitch black, the only light coming from the gate where a heavy snapping sound told me our padlock had been sheared off.

The familiar rasp of the gate opening reached me and the moon appeared as if on cue to throw her spotlight on the scene. There were two of them, one holding the torch and the other one, walking towards a lorry, carrying a set of heavyweight bolt-cutters. They'd swung the gate wide and were obviously going to back into the yard itself. For one heart-stopping moment I thought they meant to load the horses straight on to their lorry, but when they drove it quietly in, I saw to my relief it was only a Transit-sized van, not a horsebox.

The second man jumped out of the driver's seat, leaving the door open and, just as the clouds extinguished the moonlight, there was a distinct crack of breaking glass. I peered in vain, but couldn't see a thing, only hear a grunt and a scraping noise as one of them climbed through the now open window. As Ben had anticipated, they removed a window pane, released the catch and then got inside to open the door. They were quick and professional and almost silent. Faint light filtering through the cloud cover picked them out, one opening wide the back doors of the van, one disappearing inside the tack-room to start bringing out the four saddles.

A loud oath from inside the store made me jump nearly out of my skin. I saw the second man rush towards the tack-room and I pushed 9...9...9... on the mobile phone buttons with fingers that were stiff and icy with fright. Charlie heard the row too and hung over his door, and even Woolf stopped snoring and scrambled to his feet. I gabbled our name and address to the police station and told them what was happening.

'Quick, please.' I begged. 'It's not just a robbery, it's a fight. A terrible fight!'

That wasn't me being dramatic, I could hear crashes and yells and the sickening sound of punches landing.

Ben was shouting, 'I've got this one, Kez. Let yours *go!* He'll kill you...'

I felt a scream of anger rise up in me and I slid the bolt and stepped out of Charlie's stable. I hesitated for a moment, the sounds coming from the tack-room were horrendous, but I knew Kez was in trouble and I had to do something.

I ran across the yard to the van, grabbed the ignition keys from the dashboard and yelled, 'Give up! You're surrounded.'

I could see into the store now. Ben's flashlight had fallen to the floor but it threw its bright light at a crazy angle across the room. He had one man pinned to the floor and was tying his hands behind him with binder twine, but the bigger, heavier thief was giving Kez a terrible time. I could see blood all over Kez's face and one eye looked dark and swollen, but he was grimly holding on to the man's arm, refusing to let go despite the blows and kicks he was getting.

At the sound of my voice, Kez threw back his head and looked at the door horror-stricken, as if he thought I was coming in to join the fight. The big man took advantage and shook himself free, then ran outside, making for the van.

Kez staggered back, wiping blood from his mouth. 'Get out of the way, Fran!' he yelled and I took him at his word and ran like a hare. The robber jumped into the driver's seat and I heard a dreadful curse as he realised the keys weren't there. I knew he couldn't see me in the dark but I was still afraid he might somehow sense where his keys were. I almost cried with relief when I heard him pounding away in the opposite direction.

I kept running though, running as fast as I could towards the house, and when the kitchen door sprang open I fell gratefully into my mum's arms.

ELEVEN

IT FELT SO wonderfully warm and comforting, it was a few moments before I noticed a heavy something pressing into my back. I stepped back and looked at my mum. She was fully dressed, the wild hair held in a plait, the light of battle in her eyes – and a great big hammer in her hands.

I did a double-take. 'What were you going to do with that?'

She looked at the hammer thoughtfully. 'I'm not sure. I got your signal' (I'd dialled our number and let it ring three times as we'd arranged) 'and rushed up to keep watch from the attic window. At first I couldn't see a thing, then the moon came out and showed you sprinting across the yard. I saw you run up to that van, and then the sky went black again. There was some sort of light in the tack-room, I could see that, and it showed a man running from there, straight towards the van. I nearly died. I thought you were still in there.'

'So you grabbed the hammer and came down to rescue me!' I laughed and hugged her again.

'It's no laughing matter, Fran. You said you'd keep out of harm's way if I let you join in tonight. What were you thinking of?'

'Kez was being beaten up,' I said succinctly. 'So I thought if I made a diversion and pinched the van keys at the same time it would be a help. I wasn't in any danger.'

'Not much!' Ben said grimly from behind me. 'I *told* you to stay put. Sorry, Jane, I didn't think things would get quite so rough. Are the police on their way, Fran?'

'I can hear them.' Kez's voice sounded muffled. 'We've left matey boy tied up in the tack-room for them. And we've got their van, of course.'

'Thanks to me, I think,' I said, annoyed they were so

put out by my joining in. 'Come on in the house till they get here.'

They both stepped into the kitchen and Mum and I gasped. Ben was dishevelled and I could see his knuckles were grazed, but Kez looked like an extra from a vampire movie. One eye had nearly closed, the lid purple and swollen, and blood from a cut above it was running in thick streaks down his face. His chin was bruised and swollen too, and his lower lip was split open, adding to the blood spattered all over his coat.

'*Now* you see why I had to do something,' I said, and Mum rushed off to get the (herbal) first-aid kit. She was gently sponging his cut eye when the sirens Kez had heard minutes before got louder, there was a screech of tyres and Ben said, 'Ah, the cavalry. I'll go and introduce them to our captive friend in the tack-room. They might want to speak to you, Kez. Are you up to it?'

''Course,' he mumbled through the swollen mouth.

The police were pretty quick and efficient, I must say. They examined the tack-room window and the van, and put things into plastic bags without disturbing finger-prints and all that kind of stuff. To our great delight they also produced, from the back of their car, the heavy figure of a sullen-looking individual whom Kez identified instantly.

'We found him running down the road. Is this the man, sir?' the young constable asked Kez respectfully. Kez nodded.

'Yes, definitely.'

'I didn't get as close as Kez but I recognise him too.' Ben glared at the brute who stared straight ahead without speaking.

The police said more officers would be along in the morning and Ben and Kez would have to make full statements. In the meantime we were not to touch anything.

Mum and I weren't really needed in the investigations because we'd only seen patchily moonlit bits of the action. I proudly presented the policemen with the keys I'd whipped from the van's ignition and they put them in a bag and made solemn notes about them. We finished patching Kez up (he refused point blank to go to a hospital or doctor) and actually managed a few hours' sleep before the pale light of a winter's morning set us about the usual chores.

I should have felt desperately tired, I suppose, but the excitement of our plan's success and the knowledge that Kez, though battered, was now definitely unbowed, kept me going. I was singing away as I scattered the hens' feed and was quite unprepared for Ben's gloomy face when it reappeared.

'What's the matter?' I followed him into the house.

'Bad news, I'm afraid.'

'Why?' both Mum and I asked indignantly. 'We've solved the thefts, caught the thieves red-handed, what could possibly be wrong?'

'The two being held at the police station,' he jerked his head wearily in the direction of town, 'they're sticking to the same story. They say last night was just an impulse, that they've never stolen any tack before. They also say they weren't tipped off by anyone about Fran's saddle or any other saddle in the past.'

'Rubbish!' Mum said vigorously, pouring him some tea. 'Have the police searched their houses? I bet they're chockablock with stolen stuff.'

'Yes, they have, and they aren't.' Ben took a swig of his tea and sighed deeply. 'Without proof, all the police can get them for is the attempted robbery of your things. The way that was carried out, they *know* these two villains were responsible for all the others but there's just no evidence.'

I gaped at him. 'And without that evidence there's still no way we can completely clear Kez of suspicion?'

'That's right. If all these two can be charged with is last night's little episode, we haven't really achieved anything.'

'Can't the police find out who's been tipping them off?' I demanded. 'Who are those two anyway? Does that give us a clue?'

He shook his head. 'Their names are Ray Turner and Martin Handley. I don't know them. They haven't lived round here long and they say they don't know anyone and no one told them anything.'

'And while they stick to that it's impossible to prove otherwise?' Mum frowned. 'What on earth can we do, Ben?'

'I don't know about you, but this morning all I'm capable of is catching up on my sleep. I've postponed my calls till this afternoon so I can grab a couple of hours.'

I'd forgotten he'd been at the station all night. Kez had earlier succumbed to our nagging and gone to bed in the spare room. Mum had given him one of his own chamomile infusions to help him sleep despite the discomfort of his injuries, and she'd bathed his face using lotions made from bay, marigold and witch hazel. I'd peeped in before going down to feed and turn out the horses, and he'd at last fallen into a deep slumber, his good-looking face so vulnerable with its patched-up cuts and bruises.

I wished fiercely I could *do* something. I prowled about the house and yard till I drove Mum mad.

'Take Charlie out and get him over those solid jumps you've been telling me about,' she ordered. 'You'll have to concentrate then and it'll take your mind off all this.'

'We've got to find out who's passing on the information about this tack,' I argued. 'Someone told this Ray and Martin about my saddle last night. If we could find that someone...'

'Just go!' She pushed me towards the door.

She was right, of course. Having to think about clearing the hefty cross-country course Kez and I had made, did take my mind off the double worry of tack theft and Charlie-ownership. We'd discovered the jumps quite recently. Coming back from the common one day, Kez had gone 'exploring' down a little-used track and we'd found a perfect set-up tucked away at the back of a dense coppice of fir trees.

You had to push your way through brambles and undergrowth, then ride for ten minutes or so in a dark, dreary bit of woodland which was, I suppose, why the path was almost unused. It was worth traversing the dull, dripping bit though, because on the other side was a brilliant little jumping valley. A dry stone wall curved its erratic way around it, and there was a stream, hedges, even the corner rails of a solid wooden fence to negotiate. We'd added a few log piles and brushwood and worked out a figure-of-eight course which involved about sixteen jumps, all a good size and mainly of solid construction.

I'd been terrified the first time Charlie and I had gone round, and even he'd looked twice at the big leap over logs which would land us right in the widest part of the stream – almost a lake.

He did it, though, and cleared everything else I rode him at. Now it was just a question of improving his speed and timing. That day I did the course backwards for a change. Not literally of course, we just started at the wall and finished with the pile of brushwood, which was getting higher and wider every time I visited the place.

I was very pleased with the way my chestnut wonder behaved again, and headed him for home at a quiet walk. We were just emerging from the dense, dark bit of woodland when an unexpected sound caught my attention and I reined Charlie in and waited in the shadows for a moment. Just ahead I could see a flash of light as the thin winter sun reflected on the surface of a crash helmet. The noise I'd heard was getting louder, the wasp-like buzzing of a scrambler motorbike.

Curious, I strained my eyes and saw a dark-clad figure disappear from view, seemingly riding the bike into the very depths of the fir trees. I turned Charlie away from our usual path and walked him over to see where the biker had gone. There was a distinct track where he'd passed, wider than one made only by bike wheels. The deep double ruts worn along this part indicated a heavy car or van had been passing this way quite regularly.

Intrigued, I followed the clearly defined path. It led us into another dark and densely overgrown section of the wood. The bike's noise had stopped and instinctively I kept Charlie close to the trees so we weren't too conspicuous. Ahead, the track widened into a clearing and there was an old woodstore or large shed of some sort. I guessed it had been used for timber storage once. It looked old, but although dilapidated there were signs that someone had done some work there recently. The windows were newly glazed and on the stout door was a heavyweight padlock, quite new and still shiny.

The bike was propped on its stand just outside but there was no sign of the rider. I slid off Charlie's back and led him quietly behind a big rhododendron, hitching his reins over a branch. Then I edged carefully forward, taking care to keep out of sight behind the bush. The helmeted figure came suddenly into sight. He'd appeared from behind the woodstore and was clearly agitated about something. He twisted the big padlock and swore aloud, then rubbed a clean patch on the window and tried peering through.

'Ray?' he called and kicked the door angrily. 'Martin hasn't left the key.'

Suddenly I knew that voice – and I knew exactly what was in the big shed. I backed away and, slipping the reins back over Charlie's head, climbed back into the saddle.

'Quiet boy,' I whispered. 'If you know how to tiptoe, do it now.'

He dropped his nose obediently and we walked on carefully, keeping well back into the trees. We would have made it if Charlie hadn't trodden squarely on a dead branch, making it crack in half, as loud as a pistol shot. I glanced fearfully over my shoulder and saw the flash of the visor as the helmeted head turned towards us. We might still have been OK if I'd kept my head and stayed still, but it was dark and spooky in that wood and I wanted to get out. Out to home and safety. Mum was there, and Ben and Kez. I could tell them what I'd seen and they'd sort it out.

I squeezed my legs hard and Charlie shot forward in surprise. The sudden movement was enough and I heard the bike's engine roar into life behind us. I abandoned the trees and we galloped like demons along the track, hearing the wasp noise fade as we got away. Thinking the panic was over, I dropped down to canter and pointed Charlie's velvet nose towards home.

Just as we were approaching the junction that would take me onto the familiar path home, the bike suddenly shot through the trees ahead and came roaring straight towards us. I wheeled Charlie sharply and thundered, terror-stricken, back towards my cross-country course valley. It was the wrong sort of terrain for a horse versus bike race. Given a reasonable surface we could have outrun the smallish bike, but it was built for this type of scramble course, and the rider was soon flying over the bumps, swerving round trees and taking short cuts that Charlie and I couldn't manage.

He was trying to push us off the narrow path, to crush

us against the grimly dark trees, to bring us crashing to the ground. He was so close now I could feel the heat from the bike's engine, smell its oily vapour and the scorching rubber of its tyres. I tried to push Charlie on but he was stumbling on the twisted roots and rabbit burrows, his flanks being lashed by branches and thorns as the bike forced us right against the belt of dense woodland. I tried kicking out at the rider, but only succeeded in losing a stirrup and Charlie lurched again and nearly fell. My hands were buried in his mane and tears of anger and fear were rolling down my face. I saw the trees begin to thin and took sudden hope.

With all my strength I pushed the brave chestnut forward and just got to the edge, nosing ahead of the bike. Charlie's ears pricked as he recognised where he was. We were still surrounded by dense wood and there was nowhere to go, but we'd entered our jumping valley, and I knew there was only one chance to shake the biker off. I galloped on and headed straight for the big pile of logs. From this angle you couldn't see the stream curving behind it and I just prayed that by the time our pursuer realised it was there it would be too late.

We reached the logs just ahead of him and I touched Charlie's sides. He took off perfectly, soaring effortlessly over the big jump. I heard a muffled curse behind us and the squeal of brakes as the rider pulled sharply out to go round the logs. He obviously thought we'd be landing on firm ground again and I could picture the grim satisfaction on his face as he slewed his machine round the log pile. As I'd hoped, there was no warning that the ground here dropped steeply away, banking sharply into the widest part of the valley's stream. He stuck a leatherbooted foot out to try and stop himself. The engine, tyres and rider all screamed as the bike flew through the air, landing with the loud and wonderful sound of an almighty splash.

Charlie, of course, had landed beautifully, collected himself and cantered smoothly up the bank the other side. I turned my head and saw the rider wallowing wetly and trying to heave the bike off his leg. I didn't stop to help. We took a wide arc, turning back the way we'd come, cleared the stream where it narrowed and made a beeline for the wood and home.

I slowed the chestnut to a walk and patted and hugged his neck:'You were wonderful, absolutely wonderful,' I told him.

His sides heaved and his neck was wet with sweat. There were grazes and a long scratch where we'd been forced against the trees, but he still stepped out OK and there was no sign of lameness. I knew the chances of that bike starting again after being dunked under water were virtually nil, but I still listened nervously as we picked our way carefully through the trees. Charlie whickered suddenly and his ears pricked forward. I held my breath in terror, then realised he'd heard something *ahead* of us. I craned my neck and saw a horse and rider, dark as the trees that surrounded them, heading straight for us.

'Kez!' My voice cracked with relief.

His teeth flashed white for a moment, in a face that was scarred and swollen.

'What on earth are you doing? You should be recovering...' I began, but he said harshly, 'I was worried to death about you.'

He swung Woolf expertly through the undergrowth to join us and looked closely at me. 'What's happened to your face, Fran?' I put a hand to my cheek and felt blood there. 'It's just a scratch. He chased us, Kez, tried to scrape us against the trees, tried to make Charlie fall.'

'What! Who? Why?'

'There's a shed.' I waved my arm wildly. 'Over there. I

followed him and he called Ray and Martin's names. They keep the stolen tack there, Kez, we've got our evidence!'

He touched my face tenderly. 'You little devil. I woke up in a real panic, knowing you were in some kind of trouble, but I didn't think you'd be galloping around out here chasing crooks. What happened? Has he fallen off his horse?'

It was my turn to stare. 'Not a horse, a scrambler, a motorbike. He chased us on a motorbike. It was...it was horrible.'

I truly didn't mean to cry, but now I realised how frightened I'd been I just couldn't stop the tears. They stung my cut face and Kez put out his hand again and gently wiped them away. 'I'll get the *balo*. I'll *get* him.'

I was still upset but couldn't help enjoying the concern in his eyes. 'He was wearing a helmet, you know. One of those with a black visor. But I knew his voice.'

'Is it Jake?' His fists were clenched. 'He's my cousin. He's family. But if it's him who's hurt you...' He stiffened suddenly and stared intently at something behind me. 'I can see him. Stay here, Fran.'

'It's not...' I began but he was moving swiftly through the trees, neck-reining Woolf to bend and swerve his supple body.

Ahead of him I could see the figure who'd chased me. He'd spotted Kez too, and throwing the bike he was pushing to the ground, had started to run through the wood. Half screaming, half sobbing he blundered through the trees, and I'm not ashamed to say I hoped he found being hunted down as horribly frightening as Charlie and I had. Woolf bore down on him relentlessly and I saw Kez throw himself from the saddle, sending earth and dead leaves flying as both men crashed to the ground.

Charlie and I followed as fast as we could, and caught up with them just as Kez was wrenching the filthy, soaked and terrified person to his feet.

'So!' I heard the anger and hatred in his voice. 'Ben was right. It *is* you.'

'Yes,' I said, looping Woolf's reins over my arm. 'That's what I tried to tell you. It's Steve.'

TWELVE

THE BLACKSMITH'S ASSISTANT was still snivelling and whining like a coward. 'Don't hit me! I didn't mean it. They made me.'

'Who did?' Kez pinned him against a tree. 'Ray? Ray Turner?'

Steve whimpered and nodded frantically. 'And Martin Handley. I met them just after they moved here and I'd started working for Ben. They said they'd get me a good bike if I helped them.'

'And you helped them by nosing round the yards you called on, finding out what tack they had and where they kept it, too.' I stared at him in disgust. 'Most of those people you stole from were Ben's friends as well as his customers.'

'I didn't steal anything,' he said quickly and tried to loosen Kez's grip.

Kez pushed him hard against the fir tree's trunk. 'Keep still. You're too chicken to do the actual thieving, that's all. You're worse than Turner and Handley if anything.'

'Look.' Steve tried an ingratiating smile. 'Let's do a deal. There's a load of stuff in the woodshed. They were going to move it tonight after they'd got the Western saddle.'

'*My* saddle,' I pointed out icily.

'Er...yes. Sorry and all that, but once I got my bike they still paid me for tipping them the wink. And the more valuable the stuff is, like your saddle, the more I get.'

'A very fair arrangement,' Kez said drily, flexing the knuckles on his free hand. 'Except for your victims, of course.'

Steve looked in horrified fascination at the strong, sinewy fist. 'Yes...well, what I was going to say is, I'll help you get the stuff out, yours'll be in there by now Fran, and we'll go fifty-fifty, except you get all yours back of course. Martin and Ray'll think they've been done by another gang.'

'I've got a better idea,' I said. 'Let's just go to the police station and you can tell them what you just told us.'

He looked frantically at Kez. 'You wouldn't do that, would you?'

'You just watch us,' Kez said with grim satisfaction.

He frogmarched the still whining Steve all the way back to our house. I walked Charlie very slowly behind them, partly to keep an eye on Steve, and partly because we were both so shaky by then we were only capable of plodding.

Because Kez literally had his hands full with Steve I led Woolf, who was a total idiot as usual. This didn't help the fragile way I was feeling. It was as though my arm was being pulled out of its socket, but it was worth all the pain and fear we'd been through when we entered the yard and saw Mum's face. She knew what the strange little procession meant right away and rushed off to wake Ben up and tell him.

He came out of the house all sleepy-eyed and tousle-haired but when he saw Steve's still soaking and dejected figure he came instantly awake and roared so loudly the cats and dogs ran for cover.

'Steve! What the hell...'

'Just as you thought.' Kez released him suddenly and he almost stumbled into the angry farrier. 'One thieves' look-out, spy, informer, whatever you like to call him.'

'I know what I would like to call him.' I would never have believed that good-natured, kindly Ben could look so blackly furious. 'You used me, abused my trust and the trust of my customers. I could...'

He stepped towards Steve, who took one look at his face and made a bolt for it. He tore across the yard, vaulted the gate and leapt almost literally into the arms of the police.

'Going somewhere, sonny?' the constable enquired.

'Take me into custody.' Steve gabbled, peering fearfully over his shoulder. 'They're going to kill me just because I got Ray and Martin to pinch their saddle.'

The policeman was very quick. 'That would be Mr Turner and Mr Handley?'

'Yes. It's them, not me. I just told them where to find it all. I can show you the stuff they've pinched recently. It's...' His mouth dropped open. 'How d'you know their names?'

'Oh, I know *all* about them now you've filled in the gaps.' The officer winked at me. 'Just coming up to see if you'd been able to get any more evidence, Miss. And this young man will do nicely.'

I couldn't help laughing at the expression on Steve's face as realisation dawned. 'It was a set-up! You took that grille off the window to test me out, Ben.'

'Wicked, aren't I?' Ben still wasn't smiling. 'And it worked. We caught your friends red-handed with Fran's saddle and all we needed was a little proof for the other thefts.'

'So thanks for leading me to it.' I *was* smiling. 'And for the offer to go halves. Wait till the rest of your gang hear that one!'

The policeman put him in his car and made efficient notes about the woodstore.

'We'll get someone there straightaway to sort that one,' he said. 'We'd have had to let the other two go without charging them if we didn't have this.'

'You'd better pick up Steve's bike too,' I said, and even to me my voice sounded funny. 'It's in the wood.'

'Right.' He glanced at me quickly. 'That'll do for now. We'll talk to you again later, when you and your horse have been attended to. You were very brave. Thank you.'

'You're welcome.' I suddenly didn't feel at all brave. My legs felt wobbly, my face hurt and I ached all over.

'Bath and bed,' Mum said and put her arm firmly round me.

'Charlie's hurt. I've got to...'

'Ben and I will do it. It's just superficial. A bit of Romany magic and he'll be as right as rain.' Kez looked at me with worried, gentle eyes. 'You do as your mum says. You've had a hell of a time.'

That summed it up pretty well I thought hazily and went unprotestingly indoors.

The bath was a heavenly, tangerine-scented dream, and after Mum had bathed my face and the bleeding arm and leg (I hadn't realised quite what a bashing I'd got from Steve's chase), I fell thankfully into bed. I slept for hours and when I woke, Ben, Kez and Mum had done everything.

Charlie's grazed and scratched flanks weren't too bad – I had taken the brunt of the contact with the tree trunks – and he was well enough to be turned out for the afternoon with the other two. They were all back in their stables now and Kez assured me that the chestnut horse was none the worse for the scrambler-versus-horse battle. I was really pleased we were being treated as heroes, Charlie and me. I'd been a bit miffed that all I got for my key-snatching action the night before was a telling-off in triplicate, but now my three favourite people were really proud of me. Mum flapped a bit and made clucking noises when I told them how I'd followed Steve, but they all agreed racing to the log pile and dumping him and his bike in the stream was a brilliant stroke.

'Whatever happened to that timid little girl I knew a few years back?' Ben teased. 'Brave as a lion now aren't you, Fran, leaping over walls and into lakes and the like.'

'That's Charlie, not me,' I said, and tried not to think about the one black cloud in our now sunny sky.

Charlie's ownership. I was still convinced that someone, somewhere was out there pining for the beautiful chestnut Firefly or Copper Haze or whatever she'd called him.

'Don't worry.' Kez could read my mind as usual. 'We're on a winning streak. We'll sort out the Charlie business soon, I promise.'

Mum hugged me. 'I think it's all right *now*. The advert's been in for ages and no one's come forward. Just forget it and enjoy him. You two were made for each other. Like one person can bring out the best in another person, you and that horse do the same.'

'Beautifully put,' Ben ruffled her hair. 'And Fran, there's a second good thing to celebrate since you solved the tack thefts. So perhaps resolving Charlie's problem will be the third.'

'What's the second?' I looked at them all.

'Kez,' Mum said, beaming.

'You mean because his name's been cleared?'

'Not just that...his future's been decided too.'

I thought for one mad moment she was going to say she was adopting him. And I definitely didn't want him as a brother!

Kez was grinning, still devastating despite closed eye and split lip. 'I'm going to work for Ben,' he said proudly. 'We've got the arrangements to make for when I leave school in a few months, but Ben says it's definite.'

'Another tailor-made partnership,' the farrier laughed and clapped his shoulder. 'As soon as I saw the way Kez handles horses I wanted to offer him the apprenticeship, but of course I couldn't renege on my agreement with Steve.'

'And now Steve's turned out to be a crook there's a

vacancy.' Mum was bouncing around the kitchen in delight.

'*And,*' Kez said, 'there's a caravan at the forge. It's beautiful, fully equipped, and Ben says I can live there.'

'Your very own *vardo,*' I smiled at him, using the Romany word he'd taught me meaning 'wagon' and 'home'. 'You lot certainly have done some sorting out while I've been asleep. It's like one of those fairy stories you read when you're a kid...and they all lived happily ever after.'

'It's just like that.' Mum nodded solemnly. 'The job and the caravan will make all the difference to you, won't they Kez?'

'All the difference,' he agreed. 'I'm truly grateful to my uncle and his family for taking me in, but it's too crowded for me.'

'You're fond of them though, aren't you?' I remembered suddenly the anguish in his face when he'd asked me if the biker was Jake.

'Oh yes. They're not like me – Uncle could never understand why his sister ran away with a gypsy – but they're kind and they did their best by me.'

'So why did you think Jake might be involved with the thefts?' Ben asked bluntly. 'I was sure it was Steve, he was ideally placed to get information, after all, and although I never caught him taking anything I always felt he was dishonest.'

'Yeah, well I *did* catch Jake pinching my stuff, didn't I?' Kez's face was rueful. 'OK, it was only some of my remedies, I know, but I thought it meant he might just be stupid enough to get in with the Ray Turner/Martin Handley kind of crowd.'

'So that's why you told him about my saddle. I wondered why you wanted to spread the news about it if Ben was so sure Steve was the one passing on information.'

'Ben was only ninety nine per cent certain.' Kez looked guilty at the thought of suspecting his cousin. 'So he agreed I was to tell the village lads as well. The main thing was to catch the thieves themselves.'

'I saw Steve's face when he saw that Western saddle,' Ben said grimly. 'I'd have put money on it being him, but Kez wasn't so sure. We thought the two we'd caught would come up with the name, but of course in the end it was you who found Steve out.'

'Just luck,' I said modestly. 'And Charlie, of course. I suppose Steve went along to the store to gloat over my saddle. He wouldn't know his thieving friends were in jail,would he?'

'Exactly, my dear Watson,' Ben beamed at me and Mum said 'Elementary. That's what Holmes used to say.'

'Really?' I kept a straight face. 'Tell me, Ben, who was the creator of this Sherlock Holmes you just quoted?'

He caught on straightaway. 'Dickens? Or was it Shakespeare?'

'It was Sir Arthur Conan Doyle,' Mum said earnestly. 'And I always thought Conan was a good name for...' she broke off, realising we were all rocking about. 'Oh, rotten lot. You're taking the mickey. I can't help it if I find names interesting.'

She joined in the laughter, though, and I felt if only the horse I'd named Charlie was *really* my horse, life would be perfect.

We spent a few days tying up loose ends and getting details sorted out. Ben made all the arrangements for Kez to start working with him as soon as his exams were finished. Charlie and I had a really important cross-country competition coming up and were practising like mad. I was also having dressage and show-jumping lessons so that we could aim in the exciting direction of three-day eventing.

Although the evenings were getting lighter again now, I was pushed to get everything done, but when Mum announced we were going over to see Kez's caravan, I made time for that. Kez was really excited about it and showed us proudly the neatly equipped kitchen, bathroom and lounge. I liked it and I really loved the old forge. It smelt all mysterious somehow, years of iron and fire, the muscle of blacksmiths and the patience of horses.

I wandered round, looking at the lovely old harness and strange antique farming tools on the walls. Ben had a modern pinboard, too, with customers' phone numbers and clippings about other smithies and farrier news items. Some were quite interesting and I wondered if Ben's clients stopped to read the board.

'Yes, sometimes,' he said to my enquiry. 'Why? What are you thinking of?'

'I've got a copy of our advert.' I showed him the picture of Charlie. 'Could I put it up here? You never know, someone might spot it.'

'Sure.' He was co-operative as always, but I knew he thought the chances of anyone local knowing the chestnut horse were extremely slim.

I pinned the page up carefully anyway, and we went home to Mum's super-special mushroom lasagne. The next few weeks sped by, with school and homework and jumping and dressage. And fun. Mum often rode out with Kez and me now, her leg was improving daily and she was thoroughly enjoying building up the muscles by riding Brontë. The grey mare enjoyed it too, partly because Mum's so tiny, being smaller and lighter than me, and to my great amusement Brontë would often put in the odd high-spirited buck.

'She never did that with me,' I said smugly, and poor Mum shook her head in bewilderment.

'It must be my personality,' she said. 'I bring out the

naughty in horses.'

'Well, I wish you'd kept the naughty to yourself with this one,' Kez panted, struggling to keep a merrily dancing Woolf in a straight line. 'You sure your leg's not up to riding the beastly bay?'

'No fear.' Mum cantered happily away on Brontë and Charlie and I chased after her, making Woolf plunge and cavort in a frenzy of excitement.

Mum and I were laughing at the expression on Kez's face when we looked ahead and saw Ben's van bucketing slowly across the ruts toward us.

'What's he doing driving on to the common?' Mum's voice was sharp with anxiety. 'Is someone hurt or...'

Ben leaned out of the window and yelled, 'Thought I'd find you here. I phoned the house but I've got a call in the next village and I wanted you to go home straightaway.'

'Why?' I pulled up by the van's window.

'Someone's on their way round. It's the picture of Charlie. The one you put up in the forge. This chap's recognised it.'

THIRTEEN

I FELT FAINT and sick, both at once. Mum looked at my face and said quickly, 'Don't worry, Fran. Don't *worry*. We'll sort it out.'

I nodded dumbly and Kez leaned over and touched my chin. 'The third good thing, remember? It'll be all right.'

Ben grinned encouragingly. 'Of course it will.'

All three of them were doing a great job of being optimistic, but I knew how much they were worrying too.

I licked my lips which felt dry and strange. 'Who is it? Who recognised Charlie's photo?'

'A colleague of mine, I suppose you'd say. Dave's a farrier in the Midlands, comes down here on holiday sometimes and always looks me up.'

'So does Charlie belong to him?' I was holding the reins so tight my knuckles were white.

'No, no. He spotted the picture right away and is sure he put shoes on him a couple of times. I'd have my doubts with some people but Dave's got a real eye for a horse. Always remembers a quality one.'

'When was this?' Mum leaned anxiously forward to look at him.

'Not last summer, obviously, you had Charlie then, but the year before. Dave says he was called out to what he describes as a mansion on the outskirts of his town. Beautiful horse, beautiful manners, he said and he was sad that after two routine shoeings he wasn't called again.'

'Does he remember the owner?' I asked breathlessly, the picture of a sobbing, Charlie-less girl rising as always to my mind.

'Not especially. It's the horse that caught his eye. Someone rich certainly, but not one of the area's usual horsey set. Dave does remember the place was fabulous, lovely paddock and old stone stables, but the chestnut was on his own, no other horses there.'

'Oh, poor Charlie.' As usual tears sprang to my eyes. 'He'd have hated that. He loves company.'

'They all do,' Kez said, his blue eyes thoughtful. 'It sounds a funny set-up. Did this chap compete with him or what?'

'Dave can't remember,' Ben repeated. 'He thinks there was a daughter, actually, but he never saw her.'

There *was* a girl then, a girl like me, who was probably still pining for her beautiful chestnut horse.

I tried not to cry again and Kez touched my shoulder gently. 'You OK?'

I nodded, unable to speak.

Mum looked at my chalk-white face and said briskly, 'Well, at least we're going to *know*, aren't we? And if he was stolen the girl has probably got another horse by now so we'll just offer her father the proper price for Charlie.'

It was lucky I was too upset to talk I suppose, or I'd have pointed out that: (a) there was no way we could afford the proper price for a horse like Charlie, and (b) it was unlikely the girl did have another horse because Dave would be shoeing it if she had. I think they'd all worked that out for themselves anyway but were being too kind to say it. Ben turned the van round and went off to do his calls. We trailed home, not singing or talking or laughing. The horses seemed to realise how sombre and depressed we all were and even Woolf behaved himself, only shying half-heartedly at a drain once or twice.

We got back in time to see a car pull up outside our gate. Ben's friend Dave had called to see us as promised, and as soon as I saw him my heart sank to my jodhpur boots. It wasn't that he was horrible or anything, he seemed very nice in fact, but what I didn't like was the

116

look of recognition on his face when he saw Charlie.

'You're sure that's him?' Mum had done all the intro-
ductions. Like me, she'd been hoping against hope that
when the farrier saw the chestnut horse he'd say he'd
made a mistake.

'Definitely. I don't see many like that on my rounds. I
get mostly ponies and cobs, riding school hacks, that
sort. I've got a couple of decent hunter yards but this
chap stood out. You've got him looking great by the way,
better than ever.'

'Thank you,' I said dismally. 'Ben said you didn't meet
the girl who rode him, is that right?'

He frowned, his forehead crinkling into his bald head.
'I don't think I did. I'm better at horses than people, to be
honest. I know it was a lovely place, plenty of money. The
chap was there, the owner of the house, but the gardener
brought the horse in from the field if I remember. That's
right, Mr Faversham said he didn't know anything about
horses, said he left it all to his daughter.'

I bit my lip. 'What – what did she call him? What was
Charlie's name?'

He shook his shiny head. 'I don't recall, sorry Fran. I
only went out there twice. Full set both times, though I do
remember thinking the horse could hardly have been ridden, the shoes weren't worn at all.'

'So what do we do now?' Kez was all energy suddenly.
'This business has been haunting these two for months.
How can we sort it out?'

'I'll phone Mr Faversham and offer to buy Charlie.'
Mum looked really harassed. 'Perhaps he'd take money in
instalments?'

Dave shook his head again. 'I wouldn't phone him. He's
an odd sort of chap, that I do remember, and he's likely to
bite your head off. Ben's idea was to come back with me
for a day or two. I'm off home today and he's been

117

promising to come and look at my set-up for ages. He can do that and also call on the big house to see what he can find out.'

'Ben's amazing,' Mum said and looked at me and Kez. 'Isn't he? The things that man does for us is no one's business. I don't know what we'd do without him.'

'I'll tell him you said that.' Dave put his coffee mug down on the table and stood up. 'I think it'll make the trip up there worthwhile just to know he's pleased you.'

Mum blushed, I couldn't think why.

Ben left just after lunch, travelling in Dave's car to spend the night at his house in the Midlands. He planned to visit the Faversham mansion the next day and come back on the early evening train – a heck of a journey, just to help us with our problem. I thought how lucky we were, having a friend like him, and wondered vaguely if he spent as much time helping his other customers.

Kez and I drifted off to do some dung collecting in the field. Not the most cheering of chores but when you've got horses you just get on with it and it's not too bad when there's two of you. Especially if the other one is Kez.

He got the wheelbarrow and said firmly, 'Right. You've got to put it out of your mind now. We can't do anything till we know what Ben finds out, If I catch you talking about Charlie's ownership or even thinking about it I'll make you do this job without gloves or a shovel.'

'How can you tell what I'm thinking?' I giggled, despite myself. 'I might fool you by grinning like an idiot outside and fretting inside.'

'I know you well enough by now to know exactly when you're fretting.' He prodded me with the pitchfork handle. 'Anyway I'm Gypsy Kez Lee, remember? I see all, know all.'

'You are a bit of a know-all,' I agreed and shrieked when he tried to run me down with the barrow.

He kept my mind off the Charlie problem for ages, telling me stories he'd heard from his Romany granny about the old gypsy way of life.

'It's nearly gone now.' His blue, non-Romany eyes were reflective. 'There's no place for all the old crafts, peg-making, pot-mending and so on. It's hard for gypsies to earn a living the way they used to.'

'And I suppose nowadays more of them marry *gorgios* like your dad did,' I said.

'That's right. I think Gran was bitterly disappointed at that. She never became close to my mum, though she was always kind because Dad loved her so much.'

'She was close to you, though,' I said. 'She wouldn't have told you about gypsy ways and the healing herbs otherwise.'

'True.' He brought his far-away thoughts back to earth. 'Come on, then, you. Let's get practising for next week.'

That was when the chestnut horse and I were to make our eventing debut.

I shook my head and wouldn't look at him. 'What's the point? Ben might come back and tell me I've got to give Charlie back. I just can't get my heart into any training till I know.'

'OK, fair enough. Let's ride up to the common again then. Your mum's all upset now Ben and Dave have gone, we'll get her to come too.'

'All right.' I felt so restless I had to do something.

The ride was brilliant: Kez and Mum both worked so hard to entertain me, Woolf was funny and scatty, Brontë showed further signs of naughtiness, and Charlie... Charlie was perfect as usual.

We'd just crested a hill and were standing at the top, breathing in the clear air of an early spring day, when a great wave of despair washed over me. It was very nearly a year since we'd brought the scruffy scarecrow that was

Charlie back home with us, and today might be the last time I ever rode the beautiful, gleaming treasure he'd become.

I couldn't join in Mum and Kez's laughter as they joked about the mock race we'd just had. Couldn't talk. Couldn't do anything except stroke and stroke the chestnut neck, trying to fight the down tears that just wouldn't stay away. Kez looked up sharply and understood immediately.

He leaned over and touched my stroking hand. 'It'll be all right. I know it will.'

My depression lifted. He really *did* know things, see things that I couldn't. Although the fear of losing Charlie didn't leave me completely, at least I didn't bawl my way through the next horribly long waiting hours. But I honestly do not know how I got through the next day. I had to go to school, which was hideous because I couldn't concentrate on anything and kept getting stern reminders about imminent exams and the work they needed. The only bits that were bearable were breaktimes which I spent whingeing to Kelly.

She'd been fascinated by the tack theft saga and was thrilled to bits when Kez's name was finally cleared. I was quite glad she was going back to California in the summer – I'm sure she'd have gone gunning for 'the great-looking Romany' if she'd been staying here. She'd already made me promise that if I took Kez over to America to visit my dad when he settled there, we'd both pop in to see her. I'd said of course we would, had a peek at the map, gauged the distance between Arizona and her home town, and felt quite relieved it was too far. As I said before, I like her, but not *that* much.

The day brightened considerably when I discovered Kez was waiting outside school when it finished. Kelly dashed over and flirted outrageously and I was happy he didn't seem to notice. He noticed me, though, and said he thought I looked a bit peaky.

'That's just how I feel.' We were walking side by side along the narrow country lane, so close our hands were touching. 'Has Mum heard from Ben?'

'No. He said he probably wouldn't phone, he'd only just have time to get everything done, and anyway...' he broke off.

'Anyway, he'd rather tell us face to face.' I was quite calm; after the unbearable tension it was going to be a relief to know at last.

He shot me a surprised look. 'I thought you'd be in a real state. That's why I came to meet you.'

'You told me it would be all right,' I reminded him. 'So that's what I've been saying to myself all day.'

He stayed all evening. We did the chores and the feeds, had our own tea and did some homework. (Kez told me later he got the lowest mark he's ever received for that particular piece of work and I had to admit mine was the same.) Mum couldn't settle to her writing either. She was working on a Romany character in her latest book and was having trouble with him. Usually she got Kez talking to get some ideas but that night she just prowled around picking things up and putting them back in the wrong places.

I removed a salt cellar from the bookcase and asked her what time she was picking Ben up from the railway station.

'Another hour yet.' She looked at her watch. 'Are you two coming with me?'

'No,' I said quickly. 'I want to learn about Charlie here, in our house.'

'OK. I know, I'll have a bath and wash my hair. Then it'll be time to go.'

She picked up the salt pot and absent-mindedly slotted

121

it into her writing desk. I waited for her to go upstairs and took it out again. Kez and I were brushing the dogs when she came back and picked up the car keys. She'd blow-dried her hair and put some make-up on.

'You look pretty.' I tried not to sound surprised.

She went quite pink. 'Thank you. I'm off then.'

'Right you are.' We were all very calm, nothing to indicate the turmoil we were feeling.

I don't know how nervous Kez and Mum were but I had jelly legs, a butterfly stomach and a pole-vaulting heart. (A very uncomfortable combination, I can tell you.) We didn't talk much, just brushed Sam and Shelley till they were smooth and shining. I even had a go at Pinter and Ayckbourn, but they were very snooty about it and went upstairs, offended. We made some hot chocolate and stoked up the fire. Spring days are lovely but it's still chilly at night. I was keeping myself calm by doing all these things but thinking that if I had to wait any longer I'd explode. Then the dogs barked and we heard car doors slam.

Kez touched my face briefly. 'Chin up. Here we go.'

He opened the door and Mum and Ben came in from the cold.

* * * * *

I could tell as soon as I saw their faces that it was all right. They were both beaming, flushed and excited look-ing. They were also holding hands which I remember thinking was quite odd.

'Hot chocolate?' Kez raised his cup. 'Or champagne?'

'Champagne definitely.' Mum laughed almost girlishly. 'Come and give me a hug, Fran.'

I bounded over and did just that and we all settled down by the fire in a great bustle of coat-taking-off, wine-pouring and dog-patting.

I turned to Ben. 'Tell me.'

He took a great gulp of his drink and said, 'Charlie's yours. Let's start with that. I'll give you the whole story, I promise, but I can't bear those great big eyes of yours looking as if they're going to overflow.'

'As if they would,' Kez said teasingly, and squeezed my hand.

I felt light-headed. Charlie was mine!

'Start at the beginning,' Mum commanded. 'And work through to the end. Nothing like my books, they always start in the middle and go sideways, but this isn't fiction.'

'It's strange enough to be,' Ben said. 'OK, here I go. I phoned Mr Faversham this morning and was lucky enough to catch him in. He's a busy man – he kept telling me that – but I said it was urgent and he agreed to give me five minutes. And five minutes was all I got. Dave was right about him being a funny piece of work.'

'Dave was right about the house too, wasn't he?' Mum put in. 'It really is a mansion.'

'Oh, it's fabulous,' Ben agreed. 'I took Dave's car up this long, sweeping drive through grounds that looked like Kew Gardens and was shown in by a butler, no less. I waited in the study, which was about the size of a ball-room, and then this fussy little fat man arrived.'

'Mr Faversham?' I was disappointed. In all my vivid imaginings I'd pictured him about seven foot tall and looking like a demon king.

'The man himself. He was quite irritated when he found out what I wanted to know. Apparently the first few months after Charlie went he received several phone calls from people the traveller had tried to sell the horse to, and he always refused to speak to them.'

'Why?' Kez looked puzzled.

'Just spite, I think. The traveller gave Faversham's

number so he'd confirm the horse was indeed his to sell.'

It took a moment for it to sink in. 'Charlie was sold to us legitimately?' I squealed. 'That awful tinker really did own him?'

'Yes, he did. I couldn't believe it at first. Faversham said the man had turned up and offered to do labouring work on some landscaping he was having done. The work he put in was very shoddy so the millionaire refused to pay him any money. Then the bloke got nasty and started threatening, said if Faversham didn't pay he'd break down his fencing and chase his horse out onto the main road.'

'The swine!' I bounced angrily on my heels.

'He's that all right, but the rich bloke wasn't any better in my opinion. He told me he had no further use for the horse so he instructed the tinker to take Charlie in lieu of payment. He even said it killed two birds with one stone, getting rid of the horse and the traveller in one easy go. He was totally disinterested in the horse's welfare and he had no intention of letting the tinker gain financially by selling it, and so he would never confirm that the man actually owned the horse.'

'And, of course, when a rough type like that tried to sell Charlie to anyone they automatically assumed the horse was stolen,' Kez sighed in disgust.

'I didn't,' Mum pointed out, rather sadly.

I hugged her. 'Neither did I. And we were right!'

Ben laughed at that. 'You were indeed. The tinker owned Charlie quite legally, so handing your house-keeping money over and getting a receipt is a proper sale transaction. And let's face it, after a winter in that man's hands the poor horse was only worth what you paid. There's no doubt, Charlie's yours and always will be.'

I hugged Mum again, then Ben and Kez and they all hugged each other and me. (Kez and Ben didn't hug each other, though, you understand.)

'I really don't get it, though,' Kez shook his head in amazement. 'Why would Faversham get rid of the horse like that? It doesn't make sense.'

'I couldn't understand it either,' Ben told him. 'And as my five minutes were up I knew I wasn't going to find out from him. I mooched around outside, went to look at the empty stables and had a bit of luck.'

'Not luck, hard work and intelligence.' Mum waved her glass and looked soppily at him, surprising me yet again.

'If you like,' he tapped her playfully on the nose. 'I found the gardener.'

Kez and I looked at each other. 'And?'

'He told me the whole story. Faversham has a daughter, a horrible spoilt brat according to this gardener, but her rich daddy absolutely dotes on her. Whatever she wants, he buys. Faversham's pretty shrewd about money in most directions – the gardener described him as very tight in fact – but with this daughter he splashes out on whatever she wants and doesn't seem to worry when she tires of it and goes on to something else. This time she went on an adventure holiday with the school and announced she'd adored the pony trekking.'

'You don't mean...' I was listening with horrified fascination.

'Yup. Her father went straight out and got her a horse. First thing he saw, the gardener said, and the most expensive. The kid didn't have a clue, slopped around the grounds a few times, then fell off one day and wouldn't have anything else to do with riding. It was summer, of course, so Charlie was turned out with plenty of grass, but being a nice chap, the gardener was worried what would happen in the winter. The poor bloke was quite pleased that the traveller had been paid off by being given the horse. He thought – sorry, Kez – that all gypsies knew about horses so Charlie would be well looked after.'

'That *balo* was no gypsy.' Kez's face was dark and angry. 'He's the sort who gives us a bad name.'

'Poor, poor Charlie.' I'd dreaded being told the daughter was crying for him, but to hear she couldn't care less about him was almost as upsetting. 'Neglected and ignored by the Favershams, then dragged round the country by that ignorant swine of a traveller. I can't bear thinking about it.'

'Don't then.' Mum kissed me embarrassingly. 'He had a dreadful time, but it's all over and he's safe and loved and cared for now.'

'And always.' I raised my half glass of wine and saluted them all. 'To Charlie.' We all clinked glasses happily. 'The third good thing. You said they happened in threes, didn't you, Kez?'

Ben coughed a little apologetically. 'Well actually, they come in fours on this occasion. At least I hope you'll think so, Fran.'

Kez was grinning broadly and Mum was looking girlish again. I stared at them uncomprehendingly.

'We're getting married!' Mum burst out, looking at me anxiously. 'Ben and I. You *are* pleased, aren't you?'

Pleased! I was flabbergasted. But very, very, *very* pleased. We toasted them getting married, then we toasted Kez's new job, then we toasted Charlie and my eventing hopes.

I got up quite shakily. 'I'll check the horses before I do any more celebrating. I can only take so much happiness!'

'And only half a glass of wine, obviously.' Kez grinned at me and hooked my arm through his. 'I'll help you. We'll give the happy couple a few minutes on their own.'

'You knew!' I accused him as we walked through the cold, clear spring night. 'You weren't a bit surprised when they said they were getting married.'

He laughed at my indignant face. 'Did you really think Ben kept calling here just to help me? Or you, come to that?'

I thought about it. 'I suppose I did. I'm amazingly thick about some things, aren't I?'

'I think you're just...amazing.' He undid the stable bolt and kissed me softly. 'Visitor for you, Charlie. It's your owner!'

I was so happy at the words *and* the kiss that I actually didn't cry. Charlie was lying down and I cuddled into his lovely warm body, smelling his sweet grainy breath and stroking his velvet nose. I whispered all the news and he seemed to listen with interest. When I got to the bit where it was definite that I owned him, I hugged him even tighter and he obligingly nuzzled my hair as if he was delighted, too. Kez had checked the others, straightened their rugs and refilled Woolf's water bucket.

'Come on, then.' He smiled over the door at us. 'You two have a lot of work to catch up on tomorrow. Big day next week, you're going to need your beauty sleep.'

We went back to the house and as I kicked off my wellies in the kitchen I squealed suddenly, 'The competition! I wanted to put on the entry form "owned *and* ridden by Fran Harper" but I still don't know his real name. Did Ben find out? Not that it matters now, I suppose. He's my Charlie and Charlie he'll stay.'

Ben laughed so much I thought he'd choke.

'What's so funny?' I asked 'Was he called Faversham's Fiery Fiend or something equally weird?'

'No, he wasn't. They weren't interested enough to change his name, so they just called him what was on his registration papers, the gardener told me.'

'What was that?' Kez was intrigued.

'He's named after an emperor,' Ben said impressively. 'An ancient emperor of the Goths or Franks, I think it is –

you'll have to ask your history teacher, Fran – the Emperor Charlemagne. Your horse is called Charlemagne. So you can guess what he's always been known as.'

'Charlie!' we all shouted.

And Charlie it was.

that it had been possible for Young to have committed these offences only because he had been released from Broadmoor. 'This release appears to have been a serious error of judgment,' he said. 'The authorities had a duty to protect Young from himself as well as a duty to protect the public. Even Young himself thinks that a prison sentence would be better than a return to Broadmoor ... in order to avoid the possibility of further tragic consequences should he ever be released.' It seems that Graham knew the extent of his obsession with poisons and that he could never be able to guarantee that he would not once again use his fellow-citizens as guinea-pigs for his lethal experiments.

Asked later by his aunt and uncle why he preferred to go to prison rather than go back to Broadmoor, he replied, 'If this is what Broadmoor did for my condition in ten years, then I'm better off in prison.' The same aunt told the *Daily Mail*: 'This was the boy they let out of Broadmoor as cured! They should never have allowed this to happen.'

And what of the staff at Hadland's? The Criminal Injuries Compensation Board awarded various sums to Young's surviving victims, who were also entitled to industrial injuries benefit from the Department of Health and Social Security. The widows of the two murder victims also received compensation. One or two of the victims left Hadland's, but others stayed; the case of the storekeeper who knew more about poisons than many a doctor was a talking point among them for many a tea-break to come over the ensuing months. But at least their tea and coffee was no longer contaminated by the dreaded 'Bovingdon bug'.

A SELECTION OF NOVELS AVAILABLE
FROM BANTAM BOOKS

THE PRICES SHOWN BELOW WERE CORRECT AT THE TIME OF GOING TO PRESS. HOWEVER TRANSWORLD PUBLISHERS RESERVE THE RIGHT TO SHOW NEW RETAIL PRICES ON COVERS WHICH MAY DIFFER FROM THOSE PREVIOUSLY ADVERTISED IN THE TEXT OR ELSEWHERE.

☐ 17510 6	A GREAT DELIVERANCE	Elizabeth George	£3.99
☐ 17511 4	PAYMENT IN BLOOD	Elizabeth George	£3.99
☐ 40074 6	THE EVIL THAT MEN DO	Georgina Lloyd	£2.99
☐ 17606 4	MOTIVE TO MURDER	Georgina Lloyd	£2.99
☐ 17605 6	ONE WAS NOT ENOUGH	Georgina Lloyd	£2.99
☐ 17602 1	SEARCH THE SHADOWS	Barbara Michaels	£2.99
☐ 17599 8	SHATTERED SILK	Barbara Michaels	£2.99
☐ 17204 2	THE SICILIAN	Mario Puzo	£3.95
☐ 17524 6	THE SPY IN QUESTION	Tim Sebastian	£3.50
☐ 40055 X	SPY SHADOW	Tim Sebastian	£3.99
☐ 17493 2	FAVOURITE SON	Steve Sohmer	£3.99
☐ 01772 2	PATRIOTS	Steve Sohmer	£4.99
☐ 17697 8	THE BLOODING	Joseph Wambaugh	£3.99
☐ 17555 6	ECHOES IN THE DARKNESS	Joseph Wambaugh	£3.99

All Corgi/Bantam Books are available at your bookshop or newsagent, or can be ordered from the following address:

Corgi/Bantam Books,
Cash Sales Department,
P.O. Box 11, Falmouth, Cornwall TR10 9EN

Please send a cheque or postal order (not currency) and allow 80p for postage and packing for the first book plus 20p for each additional book ordered up to a maximum charge of £2.00 in UK.

B.F.P.O. customers please allow 80p for the first book and 20p for each additional book.

Overseas customers, including Eire, please allow £1.50 for postage and packing for the first book, £1.00 for the second book, and 30p for each subsequent title ordered.